FACEBOOK PHANTOM

SUZANNE SANGI

If you like this book, you might like

Zombiestan by Mainak Dhar
The Right Kind of Dog by Adil Jussawalla
Shiva and the Rise of the Shadows by Kanika Dhillon
The Wordkeepers by Jash Sen
Skyserpents by Jash Sen
Daddy Come Lately by Rupa Gulab
Queen of Ice by Devika Rangachari
Talking of Muskaan by Himanjali Sankar
The Lies We Tell by Himanjali Sankar
Unbroken by Nandhika Nambi
Year of the Weeds by Siddhartha Sarma
When She Went Away by Andaleeb Wajid
When Morning Comes by Arushi Raina
Wanting Mor by Rukhsana Khan

facebook phantom

Suzanne Sangi

duckbill

An imprint of Penguin Random House

DUCKBILL BOOKS

USA | Canada | UK | Ireland | Australia
New Zealand | India | South Africa | China | Singapore

Duckbill Books is part of the Penguin Random House group of companies whose addresses can be found at global.penguinrandomhouse.com

Published by Penguin Random House India Pvt. Ltd
4th Floor, Capital Tower 1, MG Road,
Gurugram 122 002, Haryana, India

Penguin Random House India

First published by Duckbill Books 2013

This edition published in Duckbill Books by Penguin Random House India 2020

10 9 8 7 6 5 4 3 2

ISBN 9788192594842

Typeset by PrePSol Enterprises Pvt. Ltd.

Printed at Repro India Limited

www.penguin.co.in

FSC www.fsc.org MIX Paper from responsible sources FSC® C047271

This is a legitimate digitally printed version of the book and therefore might not have certain extra finishing on the cover.

Dear Sonali

I'm glad to be your friend. I promise I will not bother you if you can tell me just this one thing. Are you happy?

Love,

Omi

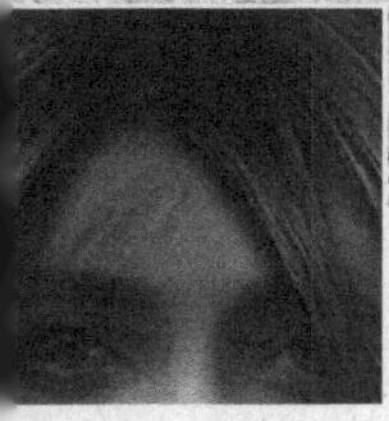

Sonali Machado

I could tell it was going to be a long day. My two very best friends, Neel and Joanne, were going on and on about Neel's birthday and some new fashion designer!

I just wasn't much of a party-lover, and my fashion sense wasn't as evolved as theirs. I quickly ran out of interest when it came to the right mix and match of tops and jeans and shoes. We were meeting after a week, and I hoped the subject would change soon.

Neel Sarathy has been my best friend since third standard. I'd stood up for him on that first day we shared one of the double desks in class. He had been a favourite target for many of the boys in the class. I guess that had actually toughened me up. We had been an inseparable duo until Joanne showed up in fifth standard. Then we became an inseparable trio.

I chewed slowly on my egg puff as we walked and I waited for the conversation to take a new turn. The new designer was coming to town and of course, would be hanging out at Debonaire, Neel's mom's totally fabulous outlet. All well-known designers in and visiting Bangalore hung out there.

'So do you wanna come see him too?' Neel asked me, breaking my trance.

'Oh, the designer guy? Is he any good?'

'Duh!' He threw a hand up in the air, exasperated. 'Haven't you been listening to anything I was saying, Li? Amazing designer? Most definitely. Hot? You have no idea, girl!'

'Of course. You would know. I believe you, Neel.' I shook my head. 'What's his name?'

Neel and Joanne rolled their eyes and replied in chorus: 'Akash Chaula.'

'Get a grip, Li. You've got to start showing some girl instincts there.' Joanne did her walking backwards thing, which she does when she wants to seriously 'look' into a person's eyes and talk to them, which was a tiny bit annoying.

'Ya! Like the ability to grasp a hot guy's name,' Neel added perkily.

'Oye! The instincts are there, alright? It's just ...' I looked up at Neel sheepishly—the guy was seriously tall, like almost six feet, though he was only turning sixteen next week. 'I am not that into fashion designers or models. I mean, some of them are seriously hot but not exactly my kind, you know.'

'Chill, Li. You don't have to worry about offending me. It's just the inconsiderate majority out there who stereotype fashion as something disgusting and unproductive, that pisses me off,' Neel finished off bitterly, but smiled kindly at me.

'Ah, touchy,' Joanne murmured.

We turned the corner and were at Neel's place.

'Look! The roses are starting to bloom, guys. This time, I can swear that I did not take help from my mom.'

He pointed to the little garden in front of his house. He loved to try his hand at different things: painting, craft, stitching and recently, gardening. He was majorly talented though he didn't make a big deal of it and people usually didn't notice.

'W-o-w!' Joanne exclaimed and clapped her hands together like a little kid. 'Damn cool, Neel. What the hell on earth can you not do?'

'That would be nothing. 'Cause hell is definitely not on earth,' Neel laughed.

'Honestly, Neel, it's beautiful! What you planning to do next?' I asked as Neel opened the door for us.

'You gonna follow the footsteps of our poet laureate here?' Joanne jerked her head towards me. Okay, I wasn't bad at poetry but the kid liked to exaggerate.

'Haha. Poetry is, unfortunately, not my *thang*, girl.'

'What. Have you given a shot at least?' Joanne did not give up.

'Well. Yeah, of course I have. But, like I said.' He shrugged his shoulders and turned the lights on.

I liked to hang out in Neel's house; we all did. I mean the three of us (that pretty much is 'all' to me). It was not very large, but comfortable. There was a sense of light, and the very modern paintings—which I could hardly understand—filled it with colour. And it was spotless 24/7.

Neel's dad had died when Neel was five. So, it was only Neel and his mom, Nita, who were the best of friends.

'Oh my god! Is tomorrow 15 April?' Joanne snapped, suddenly propping herself up on the couch.

'Yes. Obviously, Jo. A week before my birthday, 22 April. We've been talking about it the whole day!' Neel seemed kind of offended.

'Oh crap. First day of my music classes with Godzilla!' she moaned, hitting her head on the soft couch.

'You're not seriously going there, are you?!' I asked with pity.

Godzilla was the nickname of our music teacher at school, Mrs Preksha. Joanne's parents had insisted she go for extra classes with her, though Joanne had begged and moaned that she wanted any other teacher. We had just finished our tenth standard exams, and Joanne's parents felt that she would spend all her days being idle unless she attended these classes. They were not usually control freaks, but this summer had some nasty surprises.

'Yes. I. Am. Going,' she muttered feebly.

'Aww … don't worry, hon,' Neel chimed in. 'You've always wanted to, like, seriously learn music, right? So this is a good opportunity.'

'I know. It doesn't matter if it's Godzilla or any other hag out there. I mean, she's not that bad, you know …' I trailed off.

'Except for the stinking attitude and I'll-strangle-you-if-you-don't-get-this-note look that she gives,' Joanne cut me off before I could finish.

'She has a daughter,' said Neel, much to our surprise.

'Like, a girl?' Joanne asked dubiously.

'What the … of course, a girl. That's what *daughter* means, right?'

I started cracking up. Soon, Joanne and I were giggling hysterically.

'How did you come to know that? *We* didn't,' Joanne asked, taking a breath.

'Haha. Very funny,' Neel said dryly. 'She's just a bit older than us but I don't think she'd be too hard to get along with.'

'Do you mean to say that you actually checked out a girl?' I asked, trying to keep a straight face, which of course, I couldn't.

'Well, not exactly check out but …' he seemed to have run out of words and his face turned pink. He looked like a little kid who had been teased.

'Alright. That's enough, okay? Time out, guys. You've had enough fun with me today.' He made the T-sign with his hands and jumped on the couch between Joanne and me.

I woke up groggy. I had overslept. Again.

'Shit,' I muttered and turned off the radio on the table next to my bed, though my favourite song 'Tonight' was playing.

I reached for my cell phone from the table and checked the time. 6 pm. My already abnormal sleeping times were getting crappier.

The house was unusually quiet, which meant that my dad had not come home from work, and my mom and sis were chilling, probably watching a highly dramatic, romantic, macho and tragic serial on TV.

My phone vibrated and a message flashed across the screen. It was from Neel.

Hey Li, heard anything from Jo?

Today was her first day in music class and it must have got over by now.

Hiya Neel. Nope. Just woke up from my evnin slumber: P

Well, I'm kinda worried. She didn't reply to my texts or calls. I hope everything's alright.

That was weird. Joanne was never one to hide any kind of emotion from us, and that girl could text faster than you could say I-can't-text-right-now.

Ah. Don't worry Neel. I'm sure everything's ok. Maybe she's busy or sumthin.

I really didn't feel like worrying. I was still stiff from my nap. Besides, this was Joanne. She'd call up sooner or later. Still, I dialled her number. The hello tune cranked up and I couldn't help but smile. It was the hilarious modified version of Eminem's 'Stan', 'Christmas Stan'.

And then, after a few seconds, she picked up the phone.

'Hey Jo-Jo! What's going on, dude?'

'Hi Li. Wassup?' she asked listlessly. And her voice cracked at the end.

'Neel's been trying to reach you the whole evening. Why haven't you picked up his calls or texted him back?' I demanded.

'Listen, Li. I had a real shitty music class today. I'm really pissed. And that Godzilla's psycho daughter whipped my ass in front of a whole bunch of students!' I could feel her fuming on the other end.

'Whipped your ass?' I asked incredulously.

'She humiliated me. It was terrible, Li.' Her voice cracked again and I could swear she was crying this time.

Whoever could make a girl like Joanne cry had to be plain cruel. I felt my blood boiling.

'Hey there, Jo. Don't cry. Tell me what happened? Calm down, honey.' I tried my best to keep my voice under control. Showing anger wasn't going to help her.

'Well, classes started normally. I was introduced … and apparently I'm the only newbie at that shithole this summer. We kicked off with some basics, you know. And then Godzilla went out for the last hour, which left her daughter and a few of us.

'She told us to play what we had learnt today and twitched her little butt around like she was in charge. She told me to play too and so I did. And she started getting really nasty and making fun of me and stuff. I swear I could have yelled her head off but then Godzilla returned and I didn't want to give a bad impression on the very first day if I was going to have to endure the whole summer.' Joanne started sobbing uncontrollably.

Joanne Leslie was beautiful, smart, outspoken and I couldn't imagine anyone treating her like that. I tried to project my anger on a slightly healthier level.

'Oh my god, Jo! I'm so sorry. What the hell is wrong with that girl? Me and Neel, we'll figure something out tomorrow, okay?'

'I really appreciate that, Li. But I don't think that's … I mean … I can handle this.'

'Did you tell your parents about this?' I asked, concerned.

'Yeah, no. I mean, I told my mom but not my dad.'

'That's enough, I guess. But you can't let it happen again, okay?'

'Of course not, Li. It won't happen again. I was weak today; a bit emotional and cranky.'

'PMS?' I asked.

'Maybe. I don't know,' she gave a muffled laugh.

'Jeez. Get a calendar,' I snorted, glad that she had lightened up.

'Thank you but I'll keep such private issues to myself,' she snapped playfully.

'Alright, Jo. Just take care of yourself, okay? And I think you should call Neel. He's been worried sick.'

'Yah. I definitely should.' She sighed. 'Thanks for calling, Li.'

I gave a huge yawn and got up. How was I going to sleep tonight after three long hours of sleep in the evening? I went into the bathroom and splashed my face with some cool water, rinsed my mouth and brushed my tangled hair, and then wandered out of my room.

'Hey, you slept so long I thought you were dead.' My usually-sweet, sometimes-too-sarcastic sister Sonya greeted me, sprawling lazily on the couch as I passed by her in the sitting room.

'Unfortunately, I'm not dead,' I replied sourly.

She snorted and turned her attention back to the TV, grimacing at something on the screen.

'Ma, I'm hungry,' I announced, entering the kitchen.

She was on the phone, talking really fast, and seemed a little pissed. One of her colleagues, I guessed. Mom worked in a social institute dedicated to the welfare of women and kids. She was buried in work most of the time, but she thoroughly enjoyed it.

Interrupting my mom when she was on the phone was never a good idea (except for like a real emergency). She ignores you, gives you killer looks or yells her head off.

I opened the refrigerator and it stared back at me emptily.

'Did someone raid the fridge while I was asleep?' I grumbled, taking out half an apple. Nothing else. I closed the fridge grumpily and took a bite of my half-apple.

My mom snapped her phone shut and gave a relieved sigh. 'Huh, baby? Did you ask for something?'

'Uh. Yah. Is there anything edible in this house right now?'

She narrowed her eyes at me. 'Not right now. I'm going to start fixing dinner. Why? You're hungry so soon?' she started moving around the kitchen, taking a knife and a huge cauliflower.

'Gobi manchurian?' I asked hopefully.

'Would you like that?'

'Most definitely,' I squeezed her back and she squirmed, giggling.

'So what did you do today?' she asked, slicing the cauliflower.

'Hung around. Read. Ooh, there was an article today about a new designer who Neel's been talking about for weeks. He invited me to meet him too …'

Ma interrupted. 'But you're not going, right?' she asked sternly, her eyebrows scrunching together. Ma wasn't so keen on me hanging out in the fashion hub.

'Of course not,' I laughed. 'Where was I?'

'With the new designer.' She smiled at me and started washing the cauliflower.

'Then after lunch I slept.'

'Slept?'

She narrowed her eyes at me and I quickly muttered defensively, 'What? I was sleepy. That's not a crime, is it?'

'Of course not, but I hope you're making good use of your time,' she said matter-of-factly.

I muttered inaudibly, taking this as my cue to get out of the kitchen before she could tell me how to make use of my precious time, like I hadn't heard it enough. Jeez, this was supposed to be our summer holidays! Moreover, school was done. Literally. Neel, Jo and I were going to join the same pre-university and finish up college together.

I stood in the corridor. I could hear my sister giggling uncontrollably at something on TV, but decided to return to my room.

I didn't know what I felt like doing. I thought about the *useful* things that I could do this summer, other than hang out with Neel and Joanne (of course, no one dared mention this among the 'unproductive' activities in my list of daily activities). My mom had wanted me to learn French, which I was quite keen to do. But I had refused to start until college began.

I plodded up to my desk. I gave my spinning chair a twirl and then sat down heavily. I stretched myself and stared at my PC, which gaped back blankly, almost invitingly.

I logged into Facebook and phew! There were fifty-two notifications. Well, it had been two days since I'd gone online and I'd subscribed to the 'close friends' thingy. Post-boards and everybody was once again hooked to Facebook apparently.

I went through the list one by one, ignoring the apps, invitations and photo tags. My friend request list had 201 requests. I had stopped accepting friend requests from unknown people once my list had crossed four hundred. I quickly swept over the latest ones, seeing if there was anyone I knew.

I accepted three of the requests. One girl was from the Hindi tuition I used to go to, another was a guy I'd heard Joanne talk about, and the third—well, I thought he was really good-looking (if that was really him and not some model whose picture he had picked from somewhere and stuck as his profile picture).

When I clicked on the inbox, there were three messages from someone I didn't remember being 'friends' with.

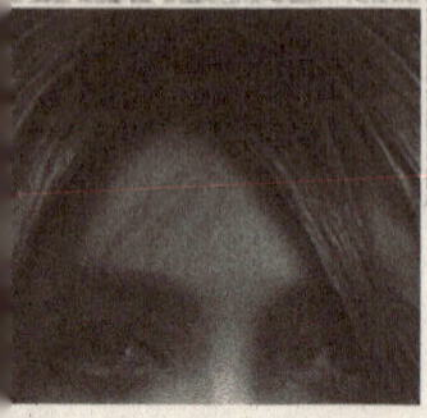

Sonali Machado

I'm glad to be your friend. I promise I will not bother you if you can tell me just this one thing. Are you happy?

I stared at it with my mouth open. What the hell was this supposed to mean? I looked at the name again. Omi Daan. Okay, I did *not* know this guy.

The message had been sent to me two days earlier, Thursday at 1:30 am. What an odd time to send such an odd message to someone who didn't even know him. He was probably one of those weirdos who bugged people with messages before actually sending a friend request.

The next message was from him again, sent a day ago.

Dear Sonali

It's me again. Are you happy?

Omi

Well, thank god he had left out the 'love' part. This was starting to freak me out. Why did it matter to him if I was happy? He didn't even know me.

Slowly I looked at the last message. I knew that it would be from him. This was sent early this morning.

I sighed, relieved that I wasn't one of those addicts who was hooked to Facebook from the break of dawn. What if I had happened to be online while he was? The messages were freaky enough; I didn't need any more of him, online, asking me if I was *happy*. I tensed as I began to read the third message.

Hello again, Sonali

I'm sorry if I'm bothering you, but I really do need to know if you're happy. I don't mean any harm to you. Just that little thing, Li. ☺

Please do reply when you get this.

Omi

He wanted to know if he was *bothering* me?! This was scaring the crap out of me! And how on earth did he know that Li was my nickname? Lucky guess? I wondered how many Sonalis out there were nicknamed Li. It was usually Sona or Sonu ... And *why* was he sooo psyched about me being *happy* or not?! The part where he said he meant no harm to me seemed to convey exactly the opposite message.

I couldn't be scared, could I? I had never even seen the guy, much less talked to him. He was just trying to have a laugh, right? I wished with all my heart that I could believe that. But something in me refused to believe. *There's something more to this*, a little part of me screamed, though I sat calmly on the chair and stared at the screen.

The best option was to ignore him. That's what my dad would have said: ignore people who seemed to threaten you and keep as far away from them as possible; this way, they will leave you alone. What if I did ignore him but he kept sending me more and more freakish and weird messages? By the looks of it, the guy didn't seem to give up that easy.

I wondered if he was a little not right in the head. Maybe that's why he was so obsessed with my being happy or not.

And then I snapped out of my daze.

Come on, he just wanted to know if I was happy or not. What harm could that mean? I shrugged away all the scary thoughts and clicked on reply.

Hello Omi

I wondered if 'Hello' was too formal, and if I should say 'Hey' or 'Hi'. But I didn't know who I was dealing with, so I stuck to formal.

It's kind of a strange message that you've sent me, you know, about me being happy or not.

I guess I am happy. I mean, no sickness or death around me so far. ☺

Okay. I was trying to be humorous. Was it humorous? I swallowed nervously.

But I want to know why it is that you're so interested in knowing such details about me.

I was trying to sound authoritative.

I thought of what else I could say. But this seemed enough. I hit the send button and watched as my message slid under his.

Okay, I couldn't take it back now. I could just wait for the guy to reply, telling me that it was all nonsense or his weird attempt to flirt with me (not that I would thaw at that), anything but the way the bizarre three messages felt.

After that, I decided to visit his profile to see if he was actually my 'friend' and also to check out what kind of a person he was (I mean, like, not *checking* out). I was just curious about him since *he* was curious about *my* happiness.

His page opened.

'Huh,' I exhaled. We were 'friends' indeed.

My eyes fell on his picture at the left-hand corner. It was bigger and clearer than the little picture in my inbox. I gasped a bit when I saw his face clearly. He was seriously good-looking; someone you could call both hot and cute. He looked seventeen, with dark hair, curly and a slight shade of bronze (I wished Neel could see him too—we both had this thing for curly hair). His eyes were a strange colour, misty grey and intense. He had a perfect nose, sharp but not too long. His lips were curved into a slight reluctant smile.

My heart sank when I saw him. After a while, I realised I felt that way because he looked sad and terribly lonely. I wondered if that was why he sent me all those messages asking me if I was happy. Maybe he just needed a friend. What he did must have been out of loneliness; it couldn't be wrong, could it?

I looked at his profile. He hadn't displayed his hometown. He was born on 15 August 1994; well, that wouldn't be easy to forget. I tried not to think about the fact that he was only a year older than me. And then my eyes went to the list of his Facebook friends.

He had only ten friends. I clicked on the list and read their names: there wasn't a single person I knew. I wondered if he was a social reject or one of those types who didn't really care. Or perhaps it was a fake account. Whichever it was, it was scary enough that I was being singled out.

I leaned back in my chair. I had been sitting up so straight that my back was aching. I stared at the picture on the screen before me. I couldn't take my eyes off his face. Something about him was compelling—I felt like there was more to him than what met the eye.

I went back to my wall. There was nothing much happening. Dorothy Ally had updated her status with the latest thought that might have run through her head (seriously, that girl updated everything that she did, what she thought, what she bought—I wonder if she had any life outside Facebook), something about her feeling lonely and miserable. A couple of guys took the opportunity to flirt and impress her with an I'm-always-there-for-you. I rolled my eyes.

Photo tags, cheesy comments, game updates, status updates; there was honestly nothing to interest me and I wondered why. Two years back, I joined Facebook. And it was the most fascinating thing ever. I logged in almost every day, taking different quizzes, playing vampire wars (yes, that was my favourite), chatting non-stop and what else, I couldn't even remember!

I wondered if I was the only one feeling this way. I didn't usually make friends, like *real* friends on Facebook, just the hi-and-bye kind. I didn't trust people's profiles if I didn't know them. I just tried to keep interaction to a minimum. I had two of the best friends in the world.

What more could I want? I did log in now and then to keep in touch with the friends I couldn't see that often. Moreover, something about Facebook made it impossible to completely forget or ignore.

A message popped in my inbox. I clicked on it. It was a new message from Omi Daan. Wow. He was fast.

Thanks for replying, Sonali.

I'm glad that you're happy. ☺

That was short.

I thought I'd asked him why he was so interested in knowing how I felt. I noticed his messages weren't through Facebook mobile but he did not show up on my chat list. Maybe we couldn't appear in each other's chat box or he kept himself offline. I was thinking of what to say in reply when another message popped in.

Okay, he was seriously into this. I wondered how annoyed I would have been if it were anyone else but him, with his curly hair, beautiful sad eyes and melancholic smile.

I would really love to get to know you, Sonali.

You have a very beautiful name, the same as my sister's ... she died seven years back. And hey! My profile picture, if you're wondering whether it's really me, it is.

Please do reply.

Love,

Omi

Oh well, there was that 'love' thing again. It didn't bother me as much as it had before and *that* bothered me. He was really polite, I noticed, his grammar perfect. Many people messaged on Facebook with abbreviations impossible to understand.

I understood why he was drawn to me. I reminded him of his sister.

A wave of sadness overwhelmed me. He must've have been crushed and it seemed like he'd been pretty close to his sister. I wondered how she had died. And then I knew what to say in reply to him.

I'm so sorry to hear that, Omi. Sure we could be friends. ☺

Well, you got a really nice profile pic.

I tried my best not to sound like I was trying to flirt, which I wasn't.

Could you tell me what happened to your sister?

I also wanted to ask if I appeared online in his chat box, but I just sent him that. I guessed he would reply after a minute or so, but he didn't.

I waited for another five minutes but got nothing. I was getting restless, even though I knew it was stupid. Sure, he could reply to the previous message, which I sent just some two minutes earlier, but he couldn't now.

After fifteen minutes, I gave up. A few chat boxes were open; few of my friends and some unknown people said hi and asked how my holidays were going. But I wasn't interested anymore. I quickly logged off, slightly pissed (which I had no reason to be). Maybe he was busy or something, I told myself. I had no right to react like this, so I tried to push the nagging thought to the back of my mind.

I switched off the computer. I thought of calling Joanne and updating her with the latest news about my new friend on Facebook (and yes, I realised I had just tried to push him to the back of my mind a few moments ago). But Joanne had enough to deal with right now; I didn't want to bother her; besides, I didn't think she'd show her usual levels of excitement in her present mood.

So I called up Neel instead. His phone rang but he didn't pick up. I tried again and after a long ring, he picked up the call.

'Hey Li,' he greeted me breathlessly.

'Hellooo,' I dragged the end, wondering if it was a bad time. 'Everything okay?'

'Yes. Why wouldn't it be?' he laughed, still trying to catch his breath.

'What are you up to?'

I could hear voices in the background, some giggling here and there. And I realised he must be in Debonaire, meeting Akash … something—I couldn't remember what his last name was.

'Are you with that Akash guy right now?' I asked, guessing where his breathlessness came from.

'Uh … yeah.' And then he whispered, like he was trying to be secretive, 'He's incredible, Li. I really wish you were here too.'

'Uh huh. Yeah, me too,' I said absentmindedly, wondering if Omi would have replied by now.

Neel seemed to sense that. Hell, he could sense anything about me.

'What about you? What are you up to?' he asked.

'Long story. Listen, I know you can't really talk now. Can you call me up later tonight? I need to tell you something.'

'Sure. But is it something serious? You can tell me now …' I heard a twinge of reluctance in his voice and decided not to deprive my best friend of his present paradise.

'That's okay, Neel. It's not an emergency. You just enjoy yourself now.'

'You sure?' he asked, a little guiltily.

'Positive. It's just some rare juicy stuff that happened today,' I added, to make sure he would get back to me. Okay, I *know* it was not something you could call 'juicy', more like 'freaky'or 'scary', but I had to get Neel's attention.

'Oooo,' he squealed. 'I'm *not* gonna sleep without calling you tonight, okay!'

'No, you won't,' I laughed at his excitement, feeling a little guilty that later he would find that what I had to tell him was not the least bit 'juicy'.

'Will you wake up, Sonali!' my sister screamed into my ear.

Why was she trying to wake me up? Didn't anybody in this house understand the concept of holidays?! You could hibernate as long as you wanted unless it was a Sunday, and you had to go to church. You could still come back *and* sleep. No one was supposed to say anything.

I refused to open my eyes and pulled the quilt tightly

over my face. Maybe if I ignored her long enough, she'd go away.

I was wrong.

'Get up! Ma's taking us to Mantri Mall now! She said we'll go today *only* if you get up now!' She wrenched harder at the quilt.

'Ma! Do something! What is wrong with her?!' she yelled louder, feigning horror.

I had to smile. I heard my mom's laughter from the hall. I understood her devious plan to get me out of bed.

'What's the time?' I asked, peeking at her.

'Ah! Li, Li, I knew it! You're not as heartless as you seem. It's already eight, da. Not that early, na?'

Everything that had happened yesterday flooded back to my mind. Omi Daan. I had been fidgety for the rest of the night, knowing that it was in anticipation of his next message but trying to deny it at the same time.

'Morning, Li.' My dad greeted me as I slouched on a chair at the dining table.

Dad was always exceptionally cheery in the mornings, the complete opposite of me. He smiled up at me from his newspaper and I returned a not-so-prompt smile.

'So, Mummy's taking you both to the mall?' he asked me as I helped myself to puri and tomato chutney.

'Yah. You coming?' I asked with my mouth full.

'No, I'll just drop you. I can get the TV to myself for a day. There's a match between Bangalore Royal Challengers and Deccan Chargers I can't miss.' He grinned like a small boy.

'I bet the whole mall that the Chargers are gonna win.'

'Yah, if you *had* the whole mall, which is as unlikely as the Chargers winning,' he snorted. 'Just go to the mall and enjoy yourself. I'll take care of the match here.' He straightened his newspaper, covering his whole face.

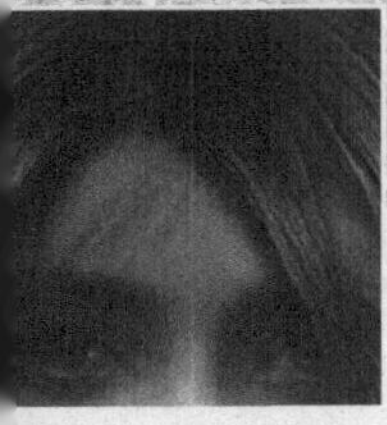

Sonali Machado

I was at the bookstore cash desk with the books I had picked when something vibrated on my butt and I jumped, making everyone around stare in my direction and then down at my butt where my hand had flown. This was embarrassing. I felt my face turn red as I yanked my phone out of my pocket.

It was Neel. *Now* he called me. Pissed, I answered the phone.

'Hey, Li. I am *so so* sorry! I swear I meant to call you back but it got really late. We only got home by one or something and … and I thought you'd be sleeping by then …'

'Of course I was sleeping by then,' I muttered, and then added in awe, 'Did you say "one or something"? Wow, that must've been some party.'

He yawned loudly. I held back a cuss—it was not like I was jealous or envious or anything but this boy had just too much fun.

'Oh no, it wasn't a party or anything. Just you know, the usual chat and a couple of drinks and ohmygosh! Akash is not only *amazing* in person but he's got this totally *to-die-for* collection which he showed us last night.'

I smiled, placing the books on the billing table. I quickly told the guy on the counter that I was waiting for my mom to get here. He nodded and I got back to Neel.

'Did you hear what I said?' he asked, still excited.

'Yep, I did. So what does he design?'

'Everything! From shoes to clothes to any kind of accessory you could dream of.' I didn't mention that was something I never actually *dreamed* of. 'He's based in Poona but he loves Bangalore, so he's thinking of settling here. My mom said she'll take him under her wing, like give him a job here so that he can have something to start with and then begin his own thing. How cool is that? Akash in Bangalore!'

'Wow! That *is* cool, Neel. But I'm thinking you should get over that guy—he's too old for you.'

'Yah, right. You haven't even *seen* him! And he is *not* old, Li.' He gave a shaky laugh.

'I didn't say he's old! I just said he's too old for you,' I muttered.

'And *why* is that getting to you?' he asked sceptically.

I blinked. What was I trying to do?

'Oh I'm so sorry, Neel. I … I'm just joking. You didn't take that seriously, did you?' What the hell was I blabbering?

'No offence … Are you okay?' Worry seemed to wipe out all his previous annoyance.

'Yah. Why wouldn't I be?' I replied quickly and tried to change the topic. I had never, once in my life, felt awkward with Neel. This was plain weird.

Ma had finished paying. I took down the books and

followed them to the table where Sonya was sitting. Ma went to get us some Pepsi.

'Okay … cool. So, you wanted to tell me something last night?' Neel asked.

I sighed in relief and hoped he didn't hear that.

'Oh yes! Dying to. I logged in on Facebook yesterday and there's this guy who had sent me three messages asking me if I was *happy*.'

'Happy?! What, he messages a hot chick like you and asks if you're *happy*? That guy's got some new techniques.' He laughed. I joined him.

'I asked him why he was so interested if I was happy or not. He replied, like, almost instantly, thanking me for replying and saying that I have a beautiful name, just like his sister who died seven years back.' I stopped to catch my breath.

'What! Ohmygosh, that is *so* sad! Maybe that's why the guy is so freaking psyched if you're happy or not. Jeesh! That's terrible, Li. What did you tell him then?' He sounded like he honestly cared, which he probably did. Neel was truly kind-hearted, one of the many things I liked about him.

'Uh … yah, I replied to him. I said I was really sorry to hear that and … I asked him what had happened to his sister. I waited for him to reply, but he didn't.'

'Oh, he must have replied by now. Where are you now? At home?'

'No, at a mall.'

'Oh well, in a few hours you can go check that out. So what does he look like, huh? You didn't tell me the main part of it.' I could picture him wagging his eyebrows, like he always did when he asked for such details.

'He's gorgeous, Neel. He's got grey eyes; I don't know if they're real but I don't think he's the kind of guy that would actually wear coloured lenses. He looks too sad, too lonely and desperate for some sugar to flavour up.' I giggled at the end.

'Oh, ya think?!' he guffawed. 'What's his name?'

'Omi Daan. You should look him up. And hey! I missed out, he's got curly hair! Yep. Beautiful, lively, curly hair.' This was it. I figured he'd be running from wherever he was, straight to his computer and signing in on Facebook.

'Whoa! You got our guy, Li. You lucky ass! I'm logging in right now.'

Just like I thought.

'You don't want your Pepsi?' Sonya asked, pointing a finger at the cup in front of me.

'Of course I do,' I snapped at her and said to Neel on the phone, 'Neel, I'll talk to you later. Text me what you think about him, okay?'

'Sure, will do that.' I could hear his hands rapidly hitting on the keys as I hung up.

I laid the books on the table. The strange part was that I wasn't eager to start reading them. Usually, my face was wedged between the pages as soon as I got a new book.

I crawled onto my bed and sat there, clutching my legs with my arms. My phone beeped, indicating that a message had been received. I ignored it. I wasn't in the mood for a texting spree.

Unable to take it any longer, I got up from the bed and sprinted to the computer.

I switched on the computer and waited impatiently for the internet homepage to open. When it did, I quickly logged into Facebook.

I could feel a jolt of happiness in me as the inbox indicated two new messages. I clicked on it and saw that both were from him.

My sister went missing for two months, after which she was found dead. We never came to know who did that to her, but I've never given up, not even today.

If I said I wanted to see you, what would you think?

Hell yeah! That's what I would think. But there was still that tiny scary part in this whole thing. I never said yes to meeting up with a stranger on Facebook, however cool they seemed. That, I felt, was a good thing. I'd heard too many stories of how something like that could lead to a *really* bad ending. The part about his sister was … heartrending. I understood his pain. If something as terrible as that happened to *my* sister … I couldn't even think of it. I opened the second message.

I won't hurt you, anyone in the world but you.

You can trust me, Sonali.

You seem to think that I'm lonely. Well, the truth is I am. I need a friend more than anything in the world and I need you to be that friend.

I cannot stop thinking about you.

Love,

Omi

Whoa! I must be dreaming. Why did he keep saying that he was not going to hurt me?

Anyone in the world but you.

Meaning that he could hurt anyone except me?! That was not a comforting thought. He wanted me to be his friend. That couldn't be so hard, could it? And the I-can't-stop-thinking-about-you part—wow!

'Same here!' I wanted to scream.

I rested my chin on my hands and thought of what to say to him.

Thanks, Omi. I have a feeling I can trust you too. ☺

Listen, you tell me when you're coming online. We'll talk then?

I sent the message. He still appeared offline. I figured it would be easier to have a real conversation if he came online. And before I could do anything else, another message arrived.

Now.

My lips curved in an expectant smile.

Omi: Hi ☺

Me: Hey ☺

Omi: How are you today, love?

Me: Great! How about you?

Omi: Ecstatic! I'm chatting with you!

Me: Heehee … I know!

Omi: So you just finished 10th std?

Me: Yep. What you doing now?

Omi: Same here. I'm only a year older than you but you must be a year smarter than me! ☺

Me: Lol! I started school at three.

Omi: Me four

Me: You see!

Omi: Yeah. So what's the scene like?

Me: Same old same old. Sleep, eat, read and then sleep. ☺

Omi: Tell me about yourself …

Me: What do you wanna know?

Omi: You ☺

I rolled my eyes.

Omi: Anything, love!

Me: Well … I'm a girl. I love books, movies, I've got two best friends … I … dunno what to say!

Omi: ☺ that's good enough … for now.

Me: How did you find me? On Facebook.

Omi: You just appeared.

Me: What do you mean?

Omi: You just appeared, love. I didn't search for you.

Me: What, someone suggested me to you?

Omi: No. You just appeared.

Me: Uh … Omi, I'm not the stupidest girl but I truly don't get what you're trying to say.

Omi: Trust me, love. Nothing is impossible.

I snorted. What did he take me for? I decided to drop it though.

Omi: You there? I'm not lying to you.

Me: Of course you're not ...

Omi: No, I'm not. What is your family like?

Me: Normal ... just mom, dad, me and my younger sister, Sonya.

Omi: You have a sister too ...

Me: Yah ... I totally understand ... you know, about your sister.

Omi: I know you do. ☺ That's why I told you.

Me: Uh ... yah ... ☺

There was this weird confidence about him, like he already knew everything about me. It was different talking to him and I liked this difference.

Me: What about your family?

Omi: Just me and my parents.

Me: Oh ...

Omi: Go on, you can ask me anything you want. ☺

Me: Oh, well ... just that.

Omi: Where do you stay?

Oops. I wished he hadn't brought up that subject.

Me: Bangalore.

Omi: I saw that, me too. But where in Bangalore?

I fumbled for the name of some place. I wasn't going to tell him my real address. Nuh-uh.

Me: Whitefield.

It was a vast area. He'd never find out that I lied, I thought smugly. Of course, unless I decided to tell him later on.

Omi: Oh that's far. I stay in RT Nagar.

I sighed in relief. That wasn't anywhere close to where I really lived. But who knew? He could be lying too.

Omi: I'm not lying.

What on earth?! Did the guy just read my mind or did he have this uncanny knack of knowing exactly what I thought.

Omi: ☺ you okay there?

Me: Yah! Why wouldn't I be?

Omi: Nothing. You just seemed to be a little thoughtful.

Me: How would you know if I was thoughtful or not?

Omi: Oh I would know.

Me: How?

I wanted to challenge him.

Omi: You're predictable.

Me: No, I'm not. We're just chatting.

Omi: 'Just' is not the word, love. This is a lot to me.

Me: Oh ... is it?

Omi: Yes. Now will you give me the opportunity to know all the little details about you that I've been dying to know?! ☺

Me: Sure! Go on, Omi! ☺

He asked me my favourite colour, my favourite books,

artists, music and food. He asked me to tell him about my family again. I had a feeling that this was what he missed the most since his sister's death. He went on to quiz me about my two best friends whom I had mentioned. I told him about Neel and Joanne.

He seemed wistful at that point, so I asked him about *his* close friends. He just said that he didn't have many friends. When I asked him why, he told me he liked to keep it that way. I didn't know how far I could believe that. That was when he cut into my thoughts again with his creepy I'm-not-lying-to-you.

I lost track of time. I remember vaguely that Ma and Sonya came into the room and went out. They must have said something to me, but I didn't hear. I was too engrossed in Omi Daan and his questions, the way he talked to me, the way he reacted to my answers, the way he commented on the little things that I said which he never ignored.

'Come and eat dinner, Sonali!' My mom's sharp voice shook me and unwillingly, I peeled my eyes off the computer screen and looked at her.

She was standing near the door, one hand on her hip and the other one pushing the curtain away from her face. I glanced at the clock and sucked my breath in shock. It was nine o'clock. Jeez! I had been online for four hours!

'Coming, Ma,' I told her sheepishly and returned to my chat with Omi, telling him that it was time for me to go.

He wished me good night and sweet dreams; I wished him the same. He asked me when I would be online next so that we could chat again. I told him it would probably be the following day, around the same time.

My heart lurched when he unexpectedly said that he would miss me till then. I could not bring myself to say that I would miss him too, even though I had a feeling that I really would.

Before I signed out, I was overcome with a desperate urge to take one last look at his wall. I clicked his name on top of the chat box and his Facebook wall opened.

He had updated the cover picture.

It was a beautiful scene in a wood. Tall sleek trees, which I couldn't put a name to, stood everywhere with sunlight pouring in from the thin top branches. I spotted a couple of green and yellow birds here and there—forest parrots, I supposed. I could feel the tranquillity and freshness of the place just by looking at the photograph.There were no people in it, so I figured it was a professional photo that he had got off the net.

I logged off and drifted to the dining room, still in a semi-trance.

I don't know what I ate. It was an unappetising meal, most of which I forced down. I returned to my room and lay on my bed, smiling up at the ceiling like a deranged person.

This was something I could *really* get used to. His name rang in my head, so did his words. I snorted, remembering that I had *actually* been scared of him initially. Stupid me. Omi Daan was an angel, sweet and kind in every way. I know that it was a lot to say after one day's chat, but I knew somehow that I wasn't wrong. I didn't think I would ever get enough of knowing him.

My phone beeped on the table. With a hint of annoyance, I grabbed it. There were four messages and three missed calls. One missed call was from Neel and the other two were from Joanne. I had totally forgotten about her! I sent her a message hastily, saying that I had been out the whole day and didn't see the calls.

One of the messages was from Joanne, asking me why I wasn't picking her call and her usual 'wazzup!' The rest of them were from Neel. I gaped at his messages, not believing what I saw.

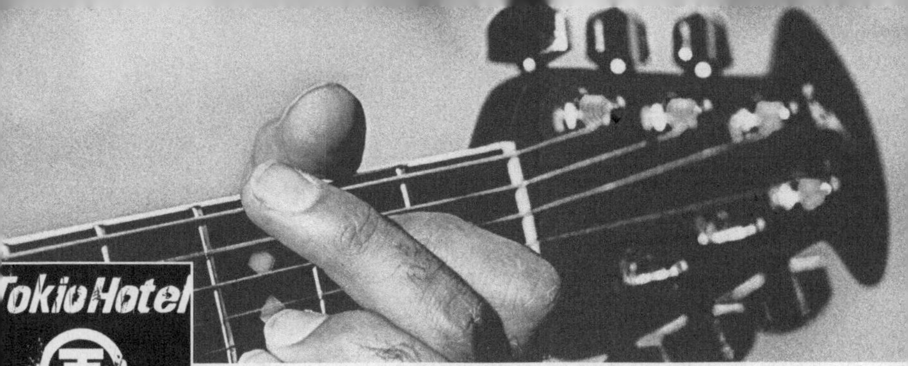

Neel Sarathy

Li. There's no Omi Daan on Facebook. I've been searching for ten minutes ... I swear there's no one like that. You sure that's the right name?!

There was no reply from the girl.

After a while and several more attempts later, I texted her again.

U there? Did you get the name right? Did I spell it wrong?

Pick up the damn call Li.

I spent several more minutes looking for him. I even checked Li's friends, scrolling patiently down her list of about five hundred friends. That girl was way too friendly.

I gave up. But the thought kept nagging me. And why was she not replying or calling?

After dinner, at about ten, I tried again.

Li, reply. I don't get it. You're not lying, are you?

After a few minutes, the phone rang. 'Hello. Li?'

'What on earth are you talking about, Neel?' She sounded like she was gritting her teeth.

'Hey, I searched, okay? There's no one called Omi Daan!'

'How can you say that! I just chatted with the guy for *four* damn hours!'

'Well … maybe I got the name wrong. Can you spell it for me?'

'O-m-i D-a-a-n.'

'That's exactly what I typed!'

'If he isn't there on Facebook, how the hell did I chat with him, Neel?!'

'Hey, *calm down*, okay? Maybe something's wrong with my computer …' I trailed off. I knew it could not be anything like that. But I did not know how to deal with this new Li.

'Neel, be rational. You know it doesn't work that way. You can't just … *not* see someone on Facebook unless he's not there!'

'Yes, there are ways, if they set their privacy listing that way. But if he is on your friends list, I should be able to see him, Li.'

'Did you look him up on my friends list?'

'Yes, that's where I first looked. He wasn't there. And then I made a general search. I still didn't find him.'

'No, it can't be. He's got to be there.' I could hear tears in her voice and the rustle of her hair against the phone. It was so easy to imagine her shaking her head and fighting back stubborn tears.

Why was she crying?

I spoke softly, as if this whole thing was not outrageously crazy. 'Okay … I'll try again.'

Silence.

'Li, you there? I'm doing it now.'

There was the rustle of her hair again. I smiled. I bet she was nodding.

'Hmm. I'm here,' she replied.

As if I had not been doing this all afternoon, I tried again. And again. I tried not to be annoyed.

I cleared my throat.

'No. I can't find him,' I said abruptly.

'Come home tomorrow. I'll show you my inbox, our chat history, everything!' she whispered.

Why was she whispering?

'Hey, hey. Sure, we'll do that. Don't worry, Li. We'll … find out.' Okay, she was definitely scaring me now.

I could hear her take a deep breath. I tried to think of something else to say. This subject was too fraught.

'Did Jo call you?' I asked.

'Huh? Yah she called but my phone wasn't with me. Did you talk to her?' She sounded kinda relieved.

'Yes, I did. Did she tell you what happened?'

'Yes, she told me, yesterday.'

'Oh, well … so, had dinner?'

'Yah, just now. What about you?'

'Yep. So I'll drop by tomorrow?'

'Yes, you definitely should,' she said. Huh. She was trying to sound so confident it was almost obnoxious.

'I'll text you when I'm coming … I'll bring Jo too. In the evening, I guess? Since you have to go to church and all …'

'Yah, perfect.'

There was a pause and she added quickly, 'You don't think I'm crazy, do you, Neel? I mean, things like this don't happen very often … do they?'

'Of course not, Li! I don't think you're crazy! Not in the slightest! No, I've never heard of such things, but there *will* be a reason; there is *always* a reason for everything, Li,' I said, making my voice sound calm.

'Oh, well. Point.'

'See, no need to get worked up at all.' I chuckled, though I did not feel amused. But I wanted to cheer her up.

I could hear the smile in her voice.

'Thanks, Neel. Are you gonna sleep now?'

'Hell no! What do you take me for, eh? I come out in the night, baby! 'Tis the nocturnal hunter's time to strike!' I laughed loudly. I knew what I was going to do that night. I was going to track down this damn Omi Daan of hers.

'Hunter, eh? What's on the menu tonight?' she giggled.

'I was just betting on my chances to get me some Ricky Martin; too bad I'd have to settle for you tonight.' I let out a dramatic sigh.

'Lol!' she chortled.

'Hey, none of those freaky *lol*s here. That's purely for online chatting or texting, 'kay?'

I hate using 'lol's when you're actually talking. Jo and Li loved to pull my leg by never missing a chance to say it.

'Yah, yah, whatever,' she snickered.

She told me all about her conversation with Omi. I deliberately ignored the fact that this guy just could not be found. I listened as if she was talking about someone real she had met, and I tried as hard as I could to be happy for my good friend Li. She is a balanced chick; I had never seen her take a header over any guy in school, though there were many who were interested in her. But she was always oblivious to the fact.

I listened like I believed every word she said. She seemed happy and almost back to her normal self.

She talked for almost an hour. And when she hung up, I turned back to my comp. I was going to find this man who was making her so happy—and I was going to make sure it was not someone playing a practical joke on her. No one messed with my Li.

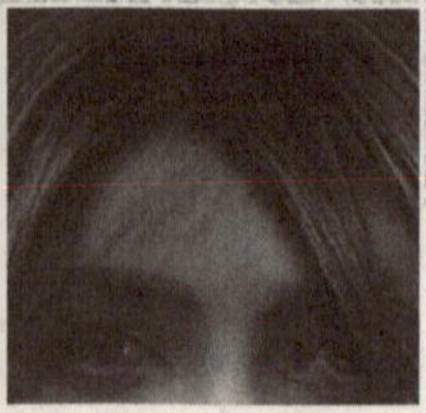

Sonali Machado

'Sonali ... Sonali ... Sonali.' Someone is calling me.

I can't remember how I got here, but I take in the beautiful scene around me. Thick, tall trees surround me, birds of various kinds, whose names I do not know, perch on them and chirp cheerily, creating a kind of musical effect. I look around me; there is not another soul. This should frighten me, but I am in bliss. The woods are so calm; the rich scents of earth and fresh air fill me and I can't even remember who I am. I have not been here before, but I have seen this scene before—I cannot remember when.

Why did someone call me? I try to ignore the annoying thought that keeps nagging at the back of my mind.

'Sonali.'

There, that voice again. 'Go away,' I want to shout, but I am unable to take my eyes off the trees, their leaves quivering with the slightest breeze.

There is a sudden gurgle of water on my left. I whip my head towards it.

A thin stream snakes deep into the woods, silver and gleaming in the sun that shines through the canopy of the trees.

I blink my eyes in disbelief; I can swear that the stream was not there a moment ago. Maybe my eyes are playing tricks on me. Like my ears—that voice has to be a hallucination since there is no one else in this part of the woods.

Where am I?

I can't possibly be dreaming, can I?

Everything around me is so lucid and real; I can feel the cool air ruffling my hair.

A fierce thirst invades my throat, more painful and urgent than anything I have ever felt. I try to swallow but it is all dry. My hands clutch my throat, trying to ease the pain.

The stream!

I try to rush to it, but my legs are rooted. I look down to see what is holding me back, but there is nothing.

I try harder, pulling, bending, but my feet won't budge!

The fire in my throat is spreading further and further down my esophagus, threatening to smoulder every part of my body.

'Help!' I try to call out but the pain is so great that it comes out as a strangled whisper. 'Help!' I try again, but the woods are empty and I know no help is going to come.

I am alone, more alone than I have ever been.

I notice through my pain that the birds have stopped chirping. They are all turned in my direction. Not a single wing is beating, their breasts heave in anticipation and their eyes remain fixed on me.

And then out of nowhere, the voice calls me again. This time it feels solid, louder and clearer than it was before and I know he is here, right next to me.

I expect to see him, though I have never heard his voice or imagined what it would be like.

Omi Daan stands a few feet away from me, his head slightly tilted, looking at me wonderingly. He looks exactly like the picture on his Facebook profile, surreal but no less perfect. His lips twitch slowly, as if he wants to smile but is unsure. Momentarily, I forget about my burning thirst as I marvel at the actual sight of him.

'Aren't you going to drink?' he asks, pointing at the stream but not taking his eyes off mine.

And then it comes back to me, the maddening thirst. I gasp and choke, still unable to move the least bit.

'Help!' I cry out to him, stretching my arms out.

He winces slightly, his eyes full of pity. He covers the distance between us in three swift strides.

He stops when he is a few inches away from me. He balls up his open hands.

I look up at him, wondering what he is planning to do. He is so tall that it hurts my neck to look up at his face.

Cold indifference replaces the warm affection on his face.

'I can't move!' I croak.

He shakes his head and his expression grows softer until he actually smiles, dazzling and kind.

'You have to get it. Yourself. Like I sought you, Sonali.'

I look at him dubiously. 'I … I don't quite understand you.'

He smiles again, making me forget what I have just said.

'You need to get that water or you'll disappear. You need to want it with all that is in you or you'll slip away, unknown and forgotten in time.' His expression is fierce but understanding.

'Wha–what are you talking about? Why am I here anyway? What's happening, Omi? Tell me!' I half-scream. My throat is hurting insanely. I try to move, but in vain.

'Come on.' He takes my hands from my throat and holds them between both his.

'Take one step at a time,' he says and pulls me gently. 'Slowly now,' he adds when my knees buckle and I almost fall on him.

And then I move! I take one step at a time as he tells me to and by the time I reach the stream, walking has become easy.

'See, I told you,' he whispers close to my ear.

I fall on my knees, scooping the cold, clear water with my shaking hands and gulping it down furiously.

I have never felt anything more satisfying in my life than that water. But the fire in my throat seems to be impossible to put out. I cannot stop drinking, even when my back hurts from bending for too long, my legs grow numb and my arms are aching from scooping up water.

I forget Omi's silent presence until he clears his throat rather loudly. I snap my head at him, glaring at his amused expression. 'What's so funny?' I grunt.

'You looked like you were about to drown,' he mutters. 'Your face is all wet.'

'I'm perfectly fine. All that talk about really wanting the water bullshit, you could've just led me here, couldn't you?'

'Yes, I could have … but you needed to know.' His tone is thoughtful and earnest.

'Know what?'

He opens his mouth to say something but shuts it again.

'Know what, Omi?' I repeat.

He looks at me full in the face and smiles. Not the dazzling, stunning smile he has given me earlier but the sad and lonely smile that makes him look so much like his picture on Facebook. His eyes look tired and old.

And then the dream ends, taking away everything it has brought with it: the trees, the birds, the stream and Omi Daan.

I opened my eyes, disoriented. Images from the dream flashed in my head. I rolled back, groaning. He had been trying to say something to me.

I kicked off my quilt and got out of bed. I couldn't wait to tell him that I had dreamt of him, I mean *sleep dream*, though the other dreaming was also true (no way I was gonna confess that yet). I glanced at the clock—it was only six-thirty. Church started at ten, so I had loads of time.

The house was quiet, which was strange for me since I usually (okay, always) woke up last, to a bustling house and high whistles of the cooker.

I washed up and combed my hair, slowly removing the tight knots. I tied a high pony and picked out a dress to wear to church. Then I sat down, wondering what to do next. Ma would be up only in another hour. So that ruled out any chances for breakfast now.

I grabbed my phone from the side table just for something to do. Joanne had not returned my calls or texted back. I sent her a quick 'hi', hoping that she was up already. Unsurprisingly she replied; Joanne was an early bird, unlike me and Neel.

I asked her if she was coming to my place in the evening with Neel. Apparently, he hadn't yet told her about it.

I managed to kill time somehow, my stomach grumbling audibly in the quiet of my room, till eight-thirty when the usual stirring of the house began.

Church service seemed endless that morning. Thoughts of Omi raced around my head erotically, however hard I tried to stop them. I kept wondering why such bizarre things were happening with him on Facebook. I couldn't wait to see if Omi would just disappear from my friends list again that evening, when I *proved* his existence to Neel and *introduced* him to Jo.

And then I thought about the dream. The place had looked vaguely familiar. Like I'd seen it in a movie or a photo …

I sat up straight, my eyes opening wide. I earned a couple of stern looks from older church members and a few curious ones from others of my age, like they'd finally found a reason to sit in church.

Omi Daan's cover picture. That was it. *That* was exactly the scene I'd seen in my dream—the woods and the birds. Well, except for the stream that had popped up from nowhere and Omi Daan, everything seemed to be exactly the same.

Whoa. This showed how obsessive I was becoming. This could not be a good thing.

When the long day at last dragged itself to four in the afternoon, my phone vibrated.

'Hi Li. How was your day?' Joanne asked merrily at the other end.

'Utterly drab and boring,' I sighed. 'How was yours?'

'Aw … sorry to hear that, girl. Mine was … Whoa! Amazing! We had some mission group which visited our church today, some really good singing, dancing. It was fun. The message was also great.'

'Nice … So when are you coming?'

'Now. I'm waiting for Neel; he said he's coming to pick me up.'

'Oh, okay. Hey, how are you feeling now?' I asked softly.

She sniggered and said, 'I'm perfectly fine, Li. Don't worry, it takes more than that to get *me* down!'

'Yah, of course!' I smiled. 'That's right, just laugh it off.'

'Alright then, see you in a few!'

I ran to the sitting room to inform my mom and dad that Neel and Jo were dropping by. The doorbell rang after twenty minutes. I darted to get the door. My dad grunted as I accidently knocked his arm, almost making him spill his tea. I managed a quick 'sorry'.

I hadn't realised that it had been drizzling till I saw Neel and Jo at the doorstep, tiny droplets of water sparkling on their hair and trickling down their faces.

'Hi!' they said at the same time.

'It's drizzling!' I squeaked in delight. I had been wishing that it would rain for days now.

'Like hell it is!' snorted Neel, wiping the water off his face with the back of his hands.

'I know! It's awesome, na? I hope it gets really heavy, man!' squealed Jo.

'So heavy that we'll be stuck here the whole evening and probably have to sleep over. Oh joy! I'm looking forward to it!' said Neel sarcastically.

'You have something against the rain? What has it ever done to you except sustain your life?' retorted Joanne, shaking her head disdainfully.

'Come on guys, get inside,' I cut in.

Jo shrugged her shoulders and walked off to say hi to my parents and Sonya who were sitting on the couch watching America's Funniest Videos.

I went to the kitchen to make tea for all of us while they burst out in laughter at some mishap. I pulled back the curtains at the kitchen windows as I waited for the milk to start boiling.

The slight drizzle had turned to a downpour. The rain battered against the open windows and sprayed through the mesh, wetting my face. I loved the rain! And the gloomy, melancholic feeling that came with it. It was very windy as well and the oak tree in front of our house swayed heavily.

I was so absorbed in gawking that I jumped when Neel said 'Hey!'

He had come just in time to stop the tea from overflowing. He quickly turned the gas stove off and blew on the tea.

'Oh shit! Nice timing, Neel,' I muttered, grabbing a spoon and stirring the tea.

'You're welcome,' he said and propped himself up on the kitchen counter.

'So ... did you talk to him today?' he asked and winked at me.

'No, I haven't gone online yet. I was saving it for when you came.'

'Sweet,' he said, cracking his knuckles.

'Oh, I'll show you *everything*!' I challenged.

He guffawed loudly and raised his hands, saying, 'Easy, easy. I never said that I didn't believe you in the first place.'

'I know but you didn't seem so convinced either.'

'Well, a computer hardly lies and neither do you. So ... it's a bit confusing to me.' He shrugged and looked at me tentatively.

'Yah, I know. That's why you're here ... and please try to get rid of that comp of yours! It's pissing and annoying and it lies!' I continued adamantly, pouring the tea into cups.

'Alright, alright. I'll burn it at the stake when you prove it wrong,' he chortled.

I arranged the cups on a tray and put out some biscuits on a plate. Neel carried the tea to the sitting room and I followed him with the biscuits.

We huddled together on the couch and had tea, laughing at the videos on TV. It felt so warm and cosy to have my friends and family crammed beside me while the wind howled and the rain sloshed outside.

After tea, Jo, Neel and I went to my room.

'Tell me everything!' said Jo as soon as I closed the door.

'Okay, here's the thing. Li's been talking to this guy on Facebook, Omi Daan,' said Neel, before I could get in a word. 'But the weird part is, I search for him but I just *can't* find him! There's nobody on Facebook called Omi Daan!'

Jo, her eyebrows scrunched, looked back and forth from Neel to me, her mouth slightly open.

'What the hell does that mean?' she asked me incredulously.

I raised my finger, slightly amused at their outraged expressions. 'It just proves that Neel's computer is bull crap.'

I quickly turned on the computer, eager to get this done with.

'Okay, let's see,' Jo said, pulling a chair close.

Neel turned here and there, clearly looking for something to make himself comfortable as well.

'Here, sit down.' I pushed the other chair towards him.

'Thanks,' he said and sat down.

I logged into Facebook.

'Check the messages; my inbox is filled with his. I'll just go get another chair,' I announced and went to the dining room to get a chair for myself.

When I returned, the both of them were staring intently at the computer, reading Omi's second message.

'He's there on Facebook alright,' muttered Neel.

Jo laughed and looked at me. 'Are you happy?' she quoted, raising her eyebrows.

'I know it's a bit freaky initially but listen, I chatted with him for *four hours* yesterday! He's actually very, very sweet,' I said defensively, squishing my chair between theirs.

'Looks like he's pretty much out of his mind to me,' shrugged Jo, clearly amused.

'Go on, read the other messages,' I prompted.

They reached the one where he told me about his sister. Jo

looked up at me, her expression had somehow softened. Neel did not look surprised; I had told him everything the night before.

'Ah … sad guy,' murmured Joanne.

Neel pursed his lips and nodded sympathetically.

I waited for them to get freaked out again when they reached the part where he said he would hurt anyone in the world but me.

'Eh? What does this mean?' asked Jo, bewildered.

'I have no idea, but it's a good thing, right?' I asked, looking back and forth between her and Neel.

'Looks exactly like what a psychopath serial killer would say,' said Neel casually and jerked his head back, pushing a strand of hair away from his face.

I narrowed my eyes at him, irritated.

'What?' he snapped. 'I have a bad feeling about this.'

'Well I think it's awesome!' said Joanne unexpectedly. 'I think it's a great opportunity for you to be something *special* for a poor lonely soul out there.' She winked at me.

Neel threw her a dirty look. 'And how special is *special*?'

'As special as I *want* it to be, alright?' I told him, sticking out my tongue at him.

'Okay, whatever.' He got up and stretched himself.

'Don't "whatever" me,' I muttered, aiming a kick at his ankle.

'Sonali!' Jo screeched suddenly, sitting up straight on the chair.

Neel and I turned to her quickly, half-expecting to see a huge caterpillar or some insect. She was pointing to the screen, her eyes shining in excitement.

I gasped in delight. There was a message from Omi in the chat box.

The first sentence was 'Hi' with a smiling emoticon; the second was 'You there?'

I grinned happily and replied.

'A bit impatient, isn't he? The "hi" was like two seconds before "you there?" How do you keep up with him, huh?' Neel asked.

I ignored him.

'Hey, we haven't even seen him clearly! Go to his page, Li,' Jo said perkily.

'Sure,' I said and clicked on his picture.

Joanne oohed; even Neel couldn't help peeking.

'Ohmygosh! How the hell did you *ever* manage to get your hands on *this*?!' exclaimed Joanne.

'Woah! He really is amazing, Li,' agreed Neel and frowned. I think he found Omi better looking than he had expected. His eyes narrowed, scrutinising appreciatively.

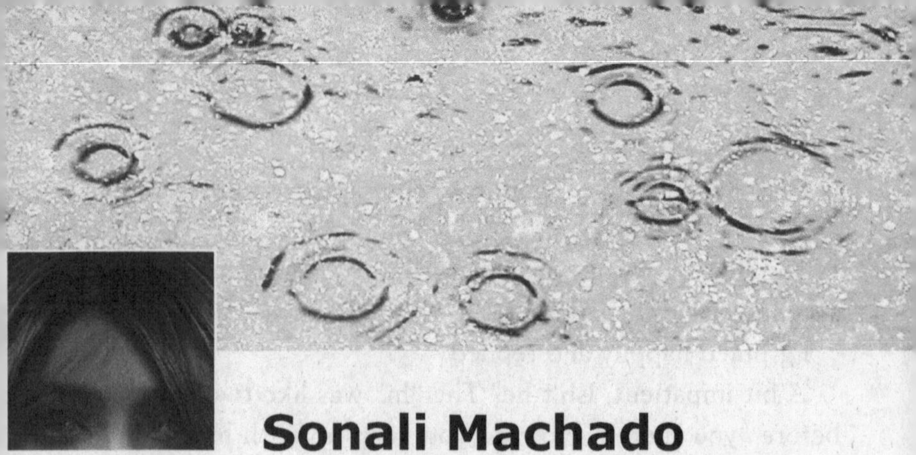

Sonali Machado

I walked Neel and Jo to the door after telling Omi that I would be back in a few seconds.

'Why take the trouble? You're anyways gonna shove us out of the door and *slam* it on our face in a few seconds,' mumbled Neel.

'Shut up, Neel,' Jo and I said at the same time.

'What's with this extremely grubby mood, huh? You hungry or horny?' Jo asked him.

Neel threw her another dirty look; I lost count of how many times he had done that throughout the evening.

'No, I'm fine, thank you,' said Neel in his calm and nasty tone.

I opened the door for them.

It wasn't raining anymore. However, the sky was dark with thunderous clouds. The wind whipped at our faces, making me shiver.

'Hey, thanks for coming by,' I told them, smiling and added, 'You know, weathering the storm for me.'

They laughed at my hyperbole.

'No problem, sweets,' said Neel, hugging me tight, a tad longer than usual.

Jo cleared her throat loudly, her hands cuffed over her mouth. 'Err, am I missing something here? Or is the weather just making you feel a little *too* cosy in there?'

'Shut up!' Neel and I snapped at her, quickly pulling apart.

'Okay, okay,' grinned Jo, throwing her hands up in the air.

I waved at them as they skittered across the road, skipping over the puddles and staying as far away as possible from the vehicles that splashed muddy water.

I sprinted back to my computer.

He had sent me a series of messages by then, asking me if I was there. Neel was right; he *was* kind of impatient, not that I didn't like this. Today I tried to get to know more about him and kept discussions about myself to a minimum.

He told me about his sister Sonali. She had looked a lot like him, except she had dark hair and black sparkly eyes like his father. He told me how she had gone missing six years back, when it seemed that everything in his life was falling apart.

He had been ten and she seven. They had gone with their parents for a springtime picnic in flower-filled Cubbon Park. It was the best day of his life, the last day that they had laughed and played as a family, whole and happy.

And then it had started to rain. His mother had held his hand tightly while his father carried Sonali in his arms, leading them towards the gate. There was a crowd of people all rushing towards the gate to get out of the rain which was getting heavier every moment.

And then something had gone wrong: Omi's father was knocked flat on the ground. He and his mother had not noticed this. When his father got back to his feet, Sonali was not in his arms any more.

'Where is she? Where is my baby?' his mother had cried out when they realised she was missing, her shrill voice piercing the rain that battered around them.

'She was—she was … here!' his father had said, his voice barely audible.

And then they had searched for her, pushing and pulling everyone around them, to have a good look, until the park was empty except for a few caretakers who ran around helplessly, trying to find a little girl whom they'd never seen in their lives.

Sonali had gone missing for two months. The police could not find her though they said they tried their best. Omi and his parents had put up flyers at every corner; around the park, their neighbourhood, near the school where he and Sonali studied. They put up the police's number as well as his father's mobile number. However, not a single person called with any news.

Two months and a week after Sonali had gone missing, they were called to the police station. They reached in haste, anticipating some lead to Sonali's whereabouts. What they had seen instead was her body, pale and lifeless.

The investigator told them that she had been found in the same park where she had gone missing. This had baffled everyone since they had searched every nook and corner of the park thoroughly. The police had been patrolling the park since that day. It would have been impossible for anyone to get inside with a dead body, and even more so, if she had been alive.

Life had never been the same after that. His family was never truly happy again. Sorrow and grief hung in the air, every hour of every day and every night. After a few months, his parents tried to make life for him as normal as they could. They stopped mentioning her name when they spoke, as though it had become taboo.

And Omi hated this. He feared that his parents would erase all memory of her. However, one day, he had seen his mother sobbing in her room, holding a picture of Sonali. His heart broke when he saw this. He swore he would find the people who murdered his sister and destroyed his mother with grief; he would find them no matter what it took.

The hours passed unnoticed. It was so easy to get lost in our own little world when Omi and I talked. I knew every little thing about his sister: the things she loved and hated, the little cloud paintings she used to make, the colour of her favourite ribbons and the games that she and Omi used to love playing. I could picture the things that he told me, picture a beautiful younger Omi laughing with his little sister.

He would ask me now and then if he was boring me, but I insisted that he go on, telling him that I enjoyed everything that he recounted; I had never meant what I said more than I meant it then. So he went on to tell me about himself; the things that he loved; his favourite food was Chinese, just like mine. His favourite band was the Backstreet Boys. I snorted at his old-fashioned taste, given the variety of mind-blowing artists around. He told me about the school he had studied in; it was somewhere in Bangalore but I had never heard of it.

I asked him if he read books; he confessed that he did not. His mother had read to him a lot when he was younger but he never actually *read* them himself.

And then I remembered my dream about him the night before! I told him everything I had seen.

Omi: Wow … you know, it's almost flattering to have you see me in your dream. I yearn for the day that it transforms to reality, Li. ☺ But it's simply absurd that I hesitated to help you even if it was just a dream! It is NEVER going happen! I want you to know that. There's just no possibility, you mean too much to me. ☺

I blushed, delighted. All my insecure feelings were suddenly brushed aside.

Me: You have no idea how fast my heart starts beating when you talk like that Omi …☺ Yes, I know that now. Well, you mean just as much to me …

Omi: As much as I absolutely loathe my dream-self for such an outrageous act, he sort of had a point, I should say … ☺

Me: A point??

From which existing angle did he have a point?

Omi: Be a sport, love ☺ but yes, I think he had a point when he said you should have tried harder to get to the water like I tried my best to get to you. ☺

I cocked my head in surprise. *How* he had got to me on Facebook was something he had been evasive about right from the start.

Me: Oh right ... then do enlighten me, Omi! Explain how you got to me.

And then, his usual comeback:

Omi: I looked for you and I found you. ☺

There were strange things about Omi—like Neel not finding him on Facebook and how quickly we had moved to such personal stuff. But glitches happen, and maybe it was the loss of his sister which made him open up to me.

It was fun, more than fun. I had never felt so happy to talk to anyone like I did to Omi, of course, that was besides Jo and Neel.

I spent hours on the computer the next few days; more often than I had ever done in the past two years. Omi seemed to be online just when I was, which was practically the whole day! I assumed that he was online even more than me, cause I always found his messages waiting for me whenever I went online, telling me that he was waiting eagerly for our next chat. We never seemed to run out of things to say. By the end of the week, he knew every little thing in my life. He could tell if I smiled or if I was upset. He had an ingenious knack for guessing the colour of my clothes and the food that I had eaten; amazingly, he was hardly ever wrong.

He never seemed to be in a bad mood, and never sulked when I was a bit moody. And I loved this about him. I had never known a kinder person, though that was a lot to say just from chatting with a person on the internet.

My phone buzzed on the bedside table. I was flat on the bed, my head buried in a pillow. My eyes were strained from staring at the computer screen for too long, making me nauseous.

I groaned and groped for the phone. The past few days, I had hardly bothered to even peek at my phone. There would be so many unanswered messages and calls by now.

The many messages and calls were mostly from Neel and Joanne, and a few from other schoolmates. My two best buddies would be pretty pissed at me. So, not bothering to open their texts, I just sent them both a message.

Hi ☺ Sorry I couldn't reply or pick ur calls … I was kinda busy, really! Sorry! Please call!

I hoped that would suffice for not responding for several days—I wasn't even sure how many.

My eye fell on the date on my phone. The following day was Neel's birthday! Shit! And I hadn't even thought of a present for him.

I jumped out of the bed but had to immediately sit down again; I felt like my head was going to explode. Seriously, I needed to cut down the time I spent on the computer by a couple of hours; my head really couldn't take any more of it.

My phone buzzed again.

'Hey! What is up with you?' Jo yelled at me.

'Hi, Jo! I'm so sorry! I was a bit … busy … with some stuff,' I replied sheepishly.

'What stuff? I've been freakin' calling you for *days*! You wouldn't pick up *or* text back!' she said, still furious.

'Yah, I know. I'm really sorry da … Listen, have you got

a gift for Neel already?' I asked in an attempt to change the subject.

'Yep, I bought it yesterday. What about you?' she asked, her voice returning to a normal octave.

'I was thinking of getting it today. And I was thinking if you could come with me,' I lied smoothly. 'You and Neel have similar tastes, you know. I wanted to get him something *really* special for his sixteenth birthday. So, what do you say, huh? You'll come with me now?'

'Sure! Why not!' she squeaked excitedly.

'Okay! I'll come by your place. You meet me at the end of your lane, right?'

'Okay. By the by, what's your budget?'

'Hmm ... Hundred-something. Hey, no pricey places, huh!'

'Sure, no problem. Come fast!'

I sighed in relief. I had remembered Neel's birthday in time and moreover, had the best shopping partner to assist me.

I rushed and got ready and darted out of my room to mom, who was sitting on the couch, watching TV with the others.

'Ma, it's Neel's birthday tomorrow. I had totally forgotten about it till today. Can I just go with Jo to get him something? I won't take long,' I told her.

She nodded, not taking her eyes off the television screen; it must have been one really interesting movie.

'Ahem!' I cleared my throat, giving her a sheepish grin.

'Oh!' she realised. 'Get my purse; it's in my room.'

She pulled out two hundred bucks and gave it to me.

'Enough?' she asked.

'Yep, thanks,' I said.

She gave me another hundred for auto fare.

'Right, thanks,' I said with a huge grin. Hundred was a lot just for auto fare—this added a nice sum to my budget for Neel's gift.

I hurried to the door. However, I paused when my hand touched the doorknob. There was that urge again! That yearning to take one last look at Omi Daan's wall on Facebook. Shopping could not be done in a jiffy. It would probably be hours before I could go online again and my phone's internet pack sucked. So I sighed, giving in and slouched back to my room, feeling like an absolute lovesick moron.

I impatiently waited for the webpage to open and logged in. No new messages.

I sighed and tried to satisfy myself by visiting his page. Well, there was *something* to see; he'd put up a new cover picture.

It was a photo of a weather-beaten bridge over a lake or river. It was dark with very scanty moonlight, making the water below glimmer in a sinisterly beautiful way. The translucent shining moon was strangely compelling.

With another sigh of disappointment, I logged off.

I got an auto pretty soon. We sped through the lane which was almost vacant, except for a few boys riding up and down on their scooters, and entered the main road.

It was rush-hour hell. I covered my nose with my hand, trying not to inhale the polluted air. It looked like it would take me at least twenty minutes to reach Jo's.

Jo was leaning against a tree, impatiently twisting her cell phone in one hand.

'Hey! You made it. I thought you would take at least half an hour to get here with the horrible traffic and all,' she called out to me as I trudged towards her.

'So I was thinking of taking you to this place where Neel took me once to check out some really cool necklaces and earrings and stuff,' she said, eyeing me with apprehension.

'Uh … you really think that'll be good enough? I mean, like he must be getting those all the time, right?'

'He gets the chains but not the earrings. He's not upgraded to *that* level yet,' she laughed but added thoughtfully, 'You're right, he must have enough of those already. Clothes then?'

'Uh-uh! Not clothes.'

'Why not?' she demanded, crossing her arms.

'Because his mom already owns a freakin' fashion outlet!' I hissed at her.

''Kay, you're right, chuck the clothes then.'

'What did *you* get for him?'

'It's a surprise,' she said and stuck out her tongue at me.

'Dude, it's *his* birthday, not mine! It's not like I'm gonna go tell him first thing tomorrow.' I scowled at her.

'Alright,' she sighed. 'I got him a pair of Converse sneakers. What do you think?'

'Wow,' I said, shaking my head in awe.

She bounced up and down on the pavement. 'Yep, shopped with Daddy that day.' She called out for an auto.

'Where you taking me?' I asked her.

She gave the auto driver directions.

'You'll see.' She told me reassuringly. 'Don't worry, I know what you're looking for.'

'Oh, do you?' I asked absentmindedly, staring at a couple of kids on the pavement. One of them looked a lot like Omi, I mused.

'Yep, you just wait and see,' she told me confidently.

I was still looking at the kid who looked so much like Omi when, suddenly, he looked straight at me.

The auto jerked to a stop, as a group of people started to cross the road. The driver swore at the top of his voice but I ignored him, and looked at the boy again.

He was looking at the people in front of us but his eyes flickered to mine as soon as I looked at him, as though he had felt my gaze upon him. I saw him clearly this time.

He looked about ten. A little girl was beside him, holding his hand firmly. I could have sworn she had not been there a minute earlier. Her jet-black hair curled thickly to her shoulders. Her eyes, marble black, sparkled as she blinked at me in curiously. The two kids resembled each other greatly and I had a feeling that they were siblings.

And then he smiled at me, deliberately, as though he had been standing there the whole day, on the side of the road, expecting to see me.

'Li?!' someone called me worriedly, yanking my arm.

Unwillingly, I turned towards the voice. It was Jo. She was staring at me.

'Are you okay?' she asked me softly.

'I'm—I'm okay. Why wouldn't I be?' I asked her, snapping my head back to where I had seen the little boy and girl.

I couldn't see them anymore. However, my eyes caught two little heads, bobbing up and down, as they raced towards a house in a narrow lane, adjacent to the main road. It was them! The boy never let go of her hand, even while opening the small gate in front of their house. He let his little sister go in first and closed the gate behind them.

'Why are you staring like that?' Joanne's freaked-out voice rang in my ears again.

'Staring at what? Why're you screaming at me?' I snapped, irritated.

'Why, you should have seen yourself! You were staring across the road at *nothing* with a really *weird* look on your face!' she hissed. Then her face softened. 'Are you not feeling well?'

'I–I'm fine, Jo,' I sighed and took her hands in mine. Then what she had said sank in. 'Wait! Did you just say that I was staring at *nothing* across the road?'

'Well, it didn't look like you were staring at *anybody* ... That look on your face was *not* normal.'

'Well, I *was* staring at someone, alright?' I muttered defensively.

'Fine,' she said, sounding a bit snubbed. 'Hey, we're almost there, just around that corner,' she told me, pointing at a tall building.

We got down from the auto and I reached into my pocket to pull out the cash. But Jo was faster.

'I brought you here; save that for the gift,' she said and pulled me towards the pavement, walking swiftly until we reached a beautifully lit gift shop. The board read Twinkles.

The inside of the shop was even more beautiful, crammed with different objects that glittered around me.

'What is this place?' I whispered to Jo in amazement.

'Twinkles,' she laughed.

I rolled my eyes at her.

I oohed and aahed as I peered around every corner. I found exactly what I wanted to give Neel Sarathy: a dreamcatcher, with multicoloured beads, designed in typical Native American style. I imagined it would hang perfectly around his neck.

I saw Jo poking around just behind me and called out to her, dangling the dreamcatcher that I had found.

'Wow! That is *so* cool, Li,' she whispered, holding the dreamcatcher tenderly in her fingers.

'I know. Hey, I'm gonna go look for something else. Just hold that, will you?' I told her and headed towards the card section.

The phone buzzed in my pocket. It was Neel.

'Hey, at last you decided to take my call, huh?' he replied grumpily to my greeting.

'I am so so sorry, Neel. I was kinda busy ... All set for tomorrow?' I hastily changed the topic.

'Yah ... kind of. You're not planning to miss out, are you?' he asked, his mood still sour.

'Of course not!'

'Hmm ... So, what are you up to?' he asked, his voice sounding lighter.

'Shopping to get something for the birthday boy!'

'Oh, really?!' he squealed in delight.

'Yep! Now can you call after an hour or something? You know how I am with gifts, so, I need to think ...'

'No, you need to *see*!' he laughed and added, 'Open your eyes, open your mind!'

The sky was darkening when I made my way back home after a small detour to Jo's place. As I sat in the auto, I thought about the boy and girl, and the eerie feeling that had crept through me when they had regarded me knowingly.

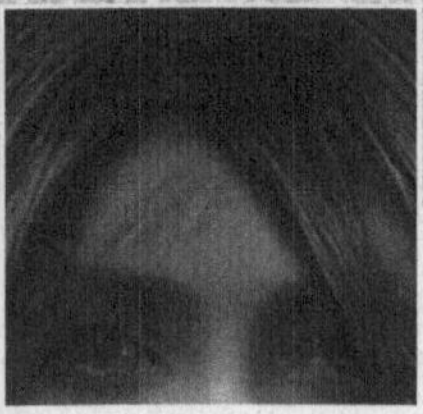

Sonali Machado

'Happy birthday!' I croaked on the phone, barely able to open my eyes.

'Thank you, Li!' Neel said happily. 'Why do you sound so sleepy? It's already ten, for goodness sakes!'

'Slept a bit late last night,' I mumbled.

'Why? Chatting with Omi Daan?'

I gave a huge yawn and replied, 'Yes.'

He made a tsk–tsk sound and sighed. 'Right. So you'll be here by four?'

'I thought celebrations start only by five-thirty.'

'Yeah, but I need some help to set things up. Jo's coming too.'

It was usually just the three of us whenever we celebrated our birthdays. Though I had been listening to Neel's elaborate party plans, I still wasn't too excited about the idea of outsiders, as I saw them, at any of our birthdays.

'Oh, sure. I'll be there.' I stifled a yawn.

'Don't be late, Li. You sound a bit tired and preoccupied by some *stuff*,' he grumbled.

'Neel, I'm not preoccupied by anything. I'll be there, *in*

time, okay?' I closed my eyes and massaged my eyeballs. 'Happy birthday again!' I said, forcing as much cheer in the sentence as I could.

Neel was always so grumpy when it came to Omi Daan. Maybe it was because of the bizarre way that Omi went missing on Facebook whenever Neel tried to find him though Omi told me he hadn't blocked anyone. Neel's attitude towards him was a bit pissing off.

I rolled back on the bed. I could grab another hour's sleep and still have more than enough time to get ready; I needed to be at his place only by four. I pulled the quilt over my face and closed my eyes.

I am standing on a huge bridge, built across a river that flows swiftly several feet below me. I shiver as a cold, dry wind hits my face and chest. My nightdress is flapping around me in all directions and I buckle my knees, trying to stop the nightdress from lifting any higher.

I can feel my body getting numb. I try to make out where I am. My eyes flit around but I cannot move my neck and body. There is no other person or creature. It is as if a plague has chased all forms of life away.

After a long, long time, out of nowhere, I hear a silent hum … that turns to a quiet whimper and then gradually grows louder and becomes a heartbreaking sob. I feel something move, a few inches away from me, though it doesn't seem to be moving towards me.

I slowly turn my eyes towards my right where the sobs seem to come from.

A small boy stands not far from me, shivering in the cold, as I am. He holds a tiny doll, with two thin braids sticking out from both sides of its head, in his arms. He seems to be trying to shield it from the cold.

'Hey!' I call out, my voice muffled.

He doesn't seem to hear me. Tears roll down his face. He clutches the doll tighter and arches over the railing of the bridge, staring vacantly at the water that gurgles below us.

And then he looks at me, full in the face. His breathing quickens and his pupils dilate in fear as he backs away from me slowly. I look back at him, confused, and panic at his reaction to my presence. I try to stretch my arms towards him and comfort him, show him that there is nothing to fear.

'Why are you here?' he calls out in a shrill voice, looking me straight in the eye. His grey eyes are piercing, and bronze curls frame a face etched with terrible loneliness.

So familiar …

'What are you doing here?' he asks me again, cautiously.

'I–I don't know … Are you alright?'

'No,' he sniffs miserably.

I try again to struggle against the invisible force that keeps me from moving. I have to go to him. I have to comfort him before he can do anything to hurt himself. I have a feeling that something terrible is going to happen soon …

He looks away from me and stares at the sky. I look up, following his gaze. The sky is as dark as the water below. A half-moon shines dimly, obscured by thick clouds that roll around lazily.

Plonk!

I snap my head down to the water to catch a glimpse of what has just fallen into the river. It is the doll. I don't understand how it can have just fallen from his hands.

My eyes dart back to him. His mouth is open in shock. His hands are outstretched towards the dark water.

And then I know what he is going to do! I have known all along! If only I had tried harder to get to him, I could have stopped him!

I watch the boy hurtling down towards the river, eyes closed and arms outstretched. Another loud plonk.

And I can see him no more as he submerges completely, without a struggle.

I woke up with a jolt, sweat pouring down my face and running down my spine. I clutched my chest, trying to calm down.

I jumped out of bed and rushed to the window, yanking open the curtains and the mesh screen. I inhaled the cool breeze and closed my eyes against the bright light, trying to shun the scenes from my dream that kept flashing before my eyes.

I glanced at the clock. It was noon. I rubbed my eyes groggily and massaged my temples, trying not to succumb to any more headaches. Going back to sleep had not been such a good idea.

Something struck me as I closed the bathroom door. Why did the little boy in my dream seem so familiar? I knew I had seen him somewhere …

Yes! It was the same boy that I had seen across the street

yesterday when Jo and I were on our way to shop for Neel's birthday present. The boy who looked like a smaller, happier version of Omi Daan, though he seemed so broken in my dream.

I splashed the cold water on my face, hoping that it would wash out the numb feeling that had filled me and the heart-wrenching scream from my dream, still echoing in my ears.

I stood before Neel's door for a few minutes longer than I had intended to. I was on time; it was five minutes past four.

I tried to compose myself, to shake off the weird feeling that had filled me since I had woken up this afternoon. The things I saw in my dreams were becoming bizarrely different. I could not explain them. I didn't even want to. The line between my dreams and the real world in which I lived was becoming too thin. The hold my dreams were beginning to have on me could *not* be a good sign.

I pressed the doorbell. Neel opened the door. He gave a huge grin when he saw me.

'Happy birthday!' I hugged him. 'Wow! Looking good.'

He was wearing black jeans and a red t-shirt with a black vest on top. He was hot, no doubt about that.

'Thanks.' He beamed. 'And you're looking *flawless*.'

I shook my head in disbelief as he hauled me inside and closed the door behind us.

'Neel! Get over here. I need longer arms to hang this thing,' Jo yelled from the sitting room.

She was balancing herself on the edge of a chair, trying to hang one end of a 'Happy Birthday Neel' banner to a nail which was slightly higher than her fingers could reach.

'Oh hey! Decided to grace us with your presence at last.' She waved at me and got down from the chair.

'Jeez. It's only four-five! Like you were here the whole morning,' I muttered, waving back at her.

'She just got here like ten minutes before you did,' said Neel, rolling his eyes and hanging the banner with ease.

Jo giggled and plopped herself on the couch.

'So, how're the preparations?' I asked, looking around the room.

The sitting room was gleaming. A long table had been placed at one corner, holding all kinds of soft drinks and alcoholic beverages. A music system with huge speakers stood at another end.

'Well, the food will arrive in a bit and then we are set,' said Neel.

'So, there's nothing much to be done now?' said Jo, crossing her legs and looking relieved.

'Nope. I guess not.' Neel shrugged his shoulders.

I gave him the present and he simply loved it—at least, it looked like he did. He wore it immediately and hastily went to put on the pair of Converse sneakers Joanne had given him.

'Where's your mom?' Jo asked, when he came back.

'She's gone to pick up a friend of hers and guess what! Her friend happens to have this *really* cute son.' Neel winked at us.

'Okay, I'm calling dibs on him!' said Jo immediately,

raising her hand. 'You have Akash, Li's got Omi and I only have *me*. So, come on, be considerate, guys.'

'Whoa! Wait. I don't exactly *have* Akash, okay. I only have a crush on him and he is *far* from mine,' said Neel, a kind of wistfulness in his voice.

'Alright then, may the best *girl* win,' Jo said sarcastically.

Jo and I giggled as Neel scowled at us.

'Come on, Jo. He's the birthday boy!'

'Chuck it, the kid's probably straight.' Neel sighed, waving his hand over his face.

The rest of the evening was a blur, once people started flooding in from around five-thirty. Most of our friends in school showed up and it was pretty much an awesome reunion. I got to see Neel's infamous Akash and he was not bad at all. Jo forgot all about the dibs she had placed on the cute son as her high-school sweetheart had shown up unexpectedly. The guy Neel was telling us about was a year older and way more gorgeous than I had expected. His name was Shivam and he seemed quite interested in me. I spent most of the evening *socialising* with him (heehee).

Music boomed from the speakers and by the end of the party, there was no one who hadn't danced. Even the adults seemed to be having a great time. Though the alcohol was kept under supervision and meant for *adults* only, Neel managed to nick some for me, Jo, Shivam and two other close friends from school. The food was also delicious; there was an array of cuisines: Indian, Chinese, Italian. I could imagine the hole in Neel's mommy's purse from all the expense.

Neel's mom dropped Jo and me home around ten. I was so tired from dancing and talking and hogging that I hit the sack immediately. But I couldn't fall asleep.

Instead, I lay on my bed and thought about Omi Daan. I hadn't spoken to him the entire day. Last night, I had told him about the little kids I had seen, who looked so much like him and his sister. He had seemed very amused and joked that I must have been hallucinating. I knew that he was just kidding but the way he said it felt a bit edgy. However, I dropped it there. I didn't want to give him the impression that I was seeing things that weren't there and moreover, I didn't want to upset him by bringing up his sister in such a sinister way.

We discussed what we wanted to do after college. He told me that he had wanted to become a CID officer ever since his sister's disappearance and death. I wasn't sure of I wanted to do. I knew what I loved to do and what I wanted to study but the actual *be* part was still variable.

There was something that I wanted to ask him. I was kind of waiting for him to bring it up but he didn't seem to be heading in that direction. I wanted to know if we could actually talk on the phone some time. I wondered if he was interested—I mean, we spoke for hours on Facebook. If he *wasn't* interested, I couldn't imagine how embarrassed I would be. But of course he would be interested, I convinced myself. By now, he knew almost everything about me. There was nothing that I couldn't tell him and I reckoned he felt the same way too. There was nothing shameful about asking him to talk to me on the phone; it was not like I was gonna ask him to meet up or something. I blushed at the thought of *actually* seeing him. No, I couldn't let my fantasies get the better of me.

I tried to stop thinking about him for a while (which was getting *extremely* rare, I realised) and instead thought about the great time I had had that evening. I tried to distract myself with how funny and insanely handsome Shivam was.

I only ended up comparing him with Omi and coming to the conclusion that he was very much like him in his politeness. I knew he had wanted to get my number after our cosy chat but I had lied to him saying I didn't have a phone. He didn't seem convinced. Of course my lie got busted when an old classmate, Cherrie, demanded why I hadn't replied to her texts that week. I mumbled something about misplacing my cell phone in some corner of the house. Neel's raised eyebrow didn't help.

Shivam didn't seem to mind. He danced with me the rest of the evening, fussed over getting food for me and flirted with me. That was flattering; I was positive that a guy as hot as him was hardly ever blown with a lie as clear as mine.

Gradually my eyelids drooped and I fell into a deep dreamless sleep.

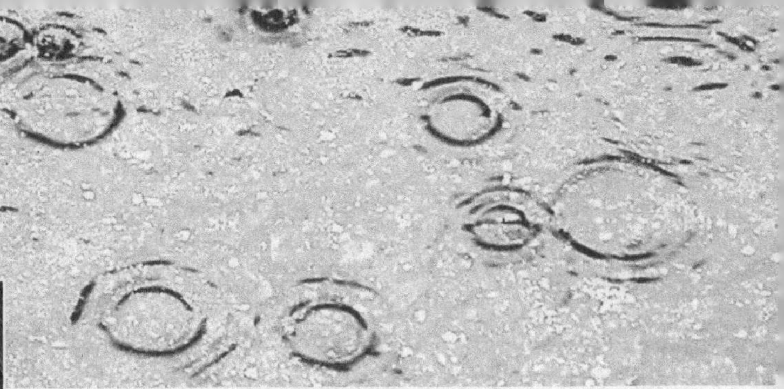

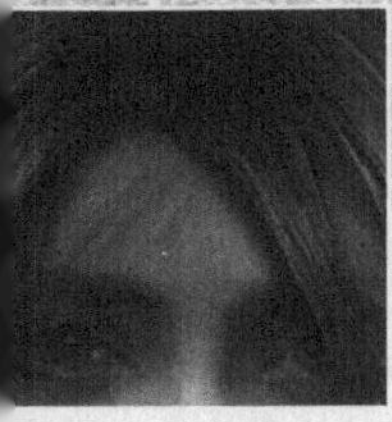

Sonali Machado

I woke up at ten-thirty, but the sky was dark and stormy and it seemed like the early hours of the morning. When I rolled over to get up, I realised Sonya was sleeping next to me. She got scared sleeping alone in her room sometimes, so she'd wedge herself between Mom and Dad or snuggle beside me.

I peered out at the rain. It seemed to have rained heavily but now it was a thin spray, the roads were slightly misty and very few vehicles passed by. I stared absentmindedly outside; the rain felt magical and soothing.

'Did you enjoy last night?' Sonya asked, making me jump.

'Yah, I had a good time.'

I went back to the bed and sat down beside her. She was still lying down, hugging my pillow.

'What were you doing? You didn't get up early as usual this morning.'

'Watched a movie that scared the shit out of me. *The Exorcism of Emily Rose*. Have you watched it?' She buried her face in the quilt.

'No,' I laughed, trying to take the quilt off her face. 'You shouldn't watch such movies late at night when I'm not there.'

'Haha, very funny,' she said dryly.

I laughed and pushed back her hair from her clammy face. It was so chill; how could she possibly sweat so much? I wondered how scared she had really been.

Breakfast was quiet that morning, each of us feeling solitary and thoughtful because of the sheeting rain and the gloomy atmosphere that it cast.

I decided to start reading one of the books I had bought last week. I started with a *House of Night* book but found myself daydreaming by the time I reached the twentieth page. I flipped the pages impatiently, wondering why I was so restless. Nothing had ever hindered an interesting book from captivating me.

I closed the book with a slam and turned on the radio, tuning in to my favourite station. A slow, mellow song drifted lazily.

'Suits the weather perfectly, no?' Sonya said appreciatively as she walked into the room.

I nodded at her.

'So, how's Omi?' she asked me, swaying her hips lightly to the rhythm of the song. She closed her eyes and glided her hands in the air.

I had told her about Omi two days back when she asked me curiously why I was suddenly so addicted to Facebook. 'I thought you liked Neel,' she had said to my surprise. Of course I quickly told her it was nothing like that. Neel was my best friend and nothing more. I wondered where she had got the impression that I, like, *liked* him.

'He's fine.' I smiled at her. 'He said hi to you.'

'Cool. Tell him I said hi too.' She smiled back at me.

She danced till the song was over and quietly left the room, saying something about a good movie that was going to air in a few minutes. She asked me if I wanted to watch it with her but I wasn't in the mood.

I sat there, thinking of how I was going to bring up the talking-on-the-phone thing the next time I spoke to Omi. What if Omi thought I was moving too fast? Was it still the boy's role to ask for a girl's number?

I wanted to talk to Jo and ask her opinion. I texted her asking her if I could call. The early bird didn't reply.

I decided to go on Facebook, wondering if Omi would be online. I thought about the dream I had had the previous afternoon. Something in me was determined to let him know about it though he couldn't possibly give a shit except maybe feel sorry that I had had a really weird dream.

I switched on the computer hastily but it took a really long time to turn on. This was unusual.

All of a sudden, the computer sprang to life, startling me. The windows quickly opened and then before I could click on anything, Google Chrome neatly opened on the Facebook homepage.

'Oh. That was fast,' I muttered, not sure if that meant something was wrong with my PC or it had turned into an incredibly smart PC.

I'd just placed my fingers on the keyboard to type in my email id when the screen went absolutely pitch black.

Shit! Now I was sure that my baby was not in normal working condition.

And that's when it blinked back to life.

My Facebook account had opened on Omi's Facebook wall with the chat box displayed.

I must have held my breath for too long because I was hit by a wave of nausea. I gripped my desk with both my hands and exhaled.

Slowly, my eyes went back to the screen and I gawked at his cover picture. It was the same gloomy one with the bridge and the water below. And then I realised what an idiot I was not to have to made this connection earlier. The bridge, the moon, the waters—everything alike, except for the boy.

My hands went limp on my lap and for a second, I felt almost ... *afraid*. Of what? I couldn't decide.

I gulped at the hard lump that was forming on my throat and then I tried to rationalise.

First things first, there was probably a virus in my computer that was responsible for the weird blackout and the sudden opening of my Facebook account. And maybe I had not logged out properly. I could probably ask Dad to take a look at it later on.

And as for the dream being the same scene as his cover picture, that could only be explained by my unhealthy obsession with Omi. I shook my head, almost embarrassed with myself.

I relaxed in the chair and checked the chat box to see if he was online.

He wasn't. There was no message either. This left me feeling hollow in a strange way. I hadn't gone online the previous day, with Neel's birthday celebration and all.

Could Omi possibly be pissed? I had told him that it was

Neel's birthday and I wouldn't be home for most of the day and he had told me to have fun and enjoy myself.

I sent him a message saying that yesterday was awesome and I couldn't wait to chat with him again. He didn't need to know the details of what had happened at the party (heehee). Anyway, what did it matter if he knew or not? It wasn't like he was my boyfriend or anything, I thought wistfully.

I sighed, staring at the screen and wishing for his chat box to pop up. But it didn't. I waited for another fifteen minutes, dismissing other Facebook friends who tried to chat with me, telling them that I was busy and would chat with them later. Omi didn't turn up, so I logged off.

I fiddled with the radio, shifting from station to station, not appeased by whatever music was playing. Irritated by my restlessness, I turned the radio off and checked the messages in my phone.

Jo had replied, telling me she was sorry for the late reply. She said she had taken a day off from music classes and was off for a picnic with her cousins.

Lucky her. I didn't reply, not wanting to spoil her obviously joyous day with my pathetic mood.

I texted Neel as a last resort knowing that he would be busy clearing up his house. However, he promptly replied. I crept back to bed and continued to read.

'Li! Guess what! I saw Omi today!' Jo half-screamed through the phone. I held the phone at a slight distance from my ear, not sure if I could believe what I was hearing.

'You serious?!' My heart pounded wildly. Fears I did not know I had were dissolving, loosening a little knot of tension in my head.

'Yes! Why would I lie? He's even more gorgeous in real, man! You should've seen him. He's ... wow.'

I felt a pang of envy as Joanne went into the details of where she saw him, how she saw him, what he wore, what he was like ... How could she see him before I did, I snarled in my head.

She and her family had driven out of Bangalore, somewhere way beyond the suburbs. It was a beautiful place, full of farms and tiny mud huts and lakes. There was an old weather-beaten bridge over a huge lake, partly dry due to the summer's heat. She had been looking out of the window when she'd seen him, with an older man and woman who could have been his parents, standing by the railing. He had been gazing at the scanty waters beneath the bridge and had looked up when the car passed, and she had recognised him.

My heart missed a beat.

I felt a bit disconcerted that he had not told me of any plans of going out of Bangalore. I wondered how right I was in believing that he told me everything about his life. But then again, we talked for hours. Every day. No, it must have been a sudden, unplanned trip that he couldn't tell me about before he left.

Moreover, there was that bizarre connection between Omi Daan standing on a bridge, looking down at the waters below and the boy in my dream who resembled him so much. I realised that I hadn't told Jo *or* Neel about my dreams. It wasn't only the dreams; I was seeing things too, like the little boy and girl on the road. I didn't want them thinking that I was hallucinating or any bullshit that questioned my sanity. I just had to work it out, compare facts with what seemed unexplainable. I didn't need them all fussing and worrying about me and my slight obsession with Omi (I guess slight was beginning to be an understatement).

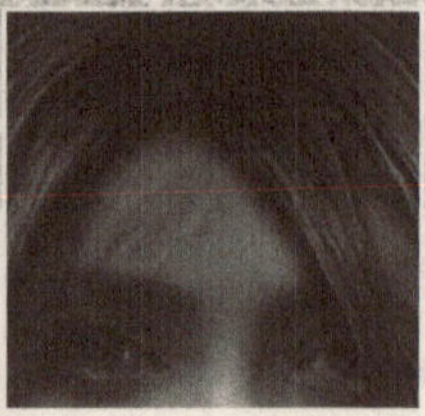

Sonali Machado

That evening, I went online again. Omi Daan was there. I told him that Jo had spotted him on a bridge in a lovely rural area. He quickly told me that it was a surprise that his parents had planned for him, a quiet family picnic.

He had gone swimming with his parents, visited a paddy field that belonged to his father's brother and just chilled. He said he missed me, sending my heart beating erratically.

I had so much to tell him. I started with the dream about the boy who had jumped off the bridge. I wanted to hear from him that it did not really mean anything, but at the same time I felt very deeply that there was a hidden truth, vague but somehow obvious. I knew I had no reason to connect him with the boy. The boy was formed in my dream and he had died in the dream itself whereas Omi had breathed and stood on the bridge just like anyone else would have.

Omi laughed it off; just like he had laughed about the little incident on the road where I had seen two kids exactly like him and his sister (at least, I thought I saw them). However, there was that edge in the way he laughed, just like before.

I could feel it—the tense way in which he dismissed it as a silly nightmare. He was evasive about matters that recalled his childhood. I could understand that so I dropped the topic soon enough. Moreover, it had been silly to connect the dream with him in the first place; I had to stop nurturing such unhealthy notions.

I tried to think of ways to bring up the talking-on-the-phone thing. And then, after our usual small talk, I asked him if we could talk on the phone sometime. I bit my lip in anticipation as he typed.

Yes.

A single 'yes'? I cocked my head, wondering if such a short reply was due to delight or because he hadn't expected me to suggest this or he was not too keen on it. I sighed, waiting for him to say more.

He didn't, so I replied.

Is there a number that I could call you on?

I chewed on my lip, trying not to let the feelings of being dejected and embarrassed creep in. There was a long pause, and then he replied.

Well actually, I don't have a phone, love. Why don't you give me your number instead so that I can call you whenever possible?

I agreed to this, though I seriously doubted that he didn't have a phone. I mean, who didn't? Completely disappointed and a little hurt at his lack of interest, I gave him my number anyway and he said thanks. I found it too formal, like something he was doing out of duty.

However, he soon proved it wrong. He told me that he couldn't wait to actually talk to me and hear my voice as soon as he got himself a phone. He remarked that I must think he was such a loser for not already having one in the first place. As odd as I found this, I waved it off and told him that it wasn't a problem. And conversation carried on.

He chatted and laughed with me, amused when I told him about the little antics I used to indulge in with my friends in high school. He himself didn't have much to share about his school days but he enjoyed my tales. The enchanted evening flew to an end, like every other evening that I spent online with Omi Daan.

His farewell for the day was as sweet and reassuring as ever. He said good night and sweet dreams, and that he would wait for our chat the next day.

I wondered if this routine would ever end. I didn't want it to. He was like my best friend but more. He could make me blush but still feel confident about myself. There was nothing in the world I couldn't share with Omi. I knew I couldn't possibly be wrong about this. Omi Daan was a completely different dimension, a safe little haven where I retired each day.

Days passed.

I spoke to Omi on Facebook. I didn't bring up talking on the phone again, and neither did he. I spoke to Jo now and then, but ignored Neel for what reasons I didn't know. He was pissed and called on my landline, demanding to know why I was acting so strange. I didn't have an answer, so I denied his accusations. This didn't help in the least and in a few days, he left me alone.

Jo asked me why I was behaving indifferently with my best friend and told me that Neel was infuriated with me. I denied it. I could feel the distance that I was creating between me and my best friends. I could feel the isolation when I stopped speaking to them. They only tried harder. They called me every day, though I never picked up the phone. They texted me. I deleted their messages even before opening them. I couldn't understand myself but I just did not want to talk to anyone.

At home, I slowly became one with the walls. Subtle as it was, it hurt more me than my withdrawal from Neel and Joanne. My parents hardly seemed to notice.

Sonya sensed it. 'Hey, what's up with you these days? Why are you always holed up in your room?' she asked.

I looked up at her after what seemed like years. Had she grown taller and rounder?

I kept gawking at her, somehow unable to give an answer until she seemed offended,

'What?' she asked, looking down self-consciously. Then she turned back to me, her face almost hostile.

I shook my head, saying nothing and then crawled into bed. I secured the quilt tightly over my head, hiding my face so that she couldn't see my desperation. I heard Sonya snort like she usually did when she felt insulted and then stomp out of my room. She didn't try to talk to me after that and I thought that strange. Sonya was not one to let go so easily. But she kept away, except to call me dutifully when lunch and dinner were ready. No more chats. No more giggling at private jokes. Nothing. I fell into that pattern soon.

My world consisted of Omi and me. I was numb to anyone else. He was my friend, brother and lover. He knew me and I knew him. His face was imprinted on my mind and his every word was like air to me. I depended on him now and he knew it. He knew how important he had become to me. And I knew he didn't take it for granted, not a single moment. I loved him with what I knew of love and he loved me with all he knew of love. And that was it. Everything else came a distant second or didn't matter at all.

'Li? Are you in there?'

I turned my head towards the door. I knew the voice; I had dreaded to hear it. I knew I had to confront it one day or another but now, hearing it so close to me, I wanted to run away as fast as my legs could carry me. I held the book in my lap gingerly, my hands shaking. I closed my eyes and waited for the door to open.

Three sharp raps on the door. Why couldn't they just come inside? They knew I was inside and they also knew that the last thing I wanted was them confronting me. I sighed when the door opened, and I heard their soft footfalls as they approached me rather cautiously. I still didn't open my eyes. I couldn't bear to look at them, after days of pretending they didn't exist. I waited for either of them to say something first. And then he spoke.

'Li. What's wrong? Tell me.' I had never heard him sound so firm and yet intensely protective. One of them placed a hand on mine and squeezed it gently, another put an arm around my waist.

I opened my eyes warily. Their expressions were not what I expected to see. There was no hint of anger or frustration or bitterness.

Jo's big eyes were full of worry and care. She hugged me though I sat as rigid as a rock. Neel was holding my hand. His jaws were set tightly and his eyebrows were scrunched in worry and confusion. I didn't know what to say to him. I looked away from them, unable to take it anymore.

'Li. We're your best friends. We know something's wrong. Please tell us, na!' Jo whispered.

Neel eyed her meaningfully; they had planned to do this as calmly as possible. It didn't matter; I wanted to tell them.

Nothing they could say was of any use right now. I was already lost. I couldn't listen to what they said even if I could hear them. They wouldn't understand. My world had changed hands many days back. I didn't own myself anymore; he did, Omi Daan.

That was it! That was all I needed to tell them, then they would leave me alone. I took a deep breath and sat up straight. I shook Jo's arms off and pulled my hand out of Neel's grip. They looked at me, waiting to hear what I had to say.

I opened my mouth but stopped short. They should have never come to see me. But they had. So they had to hear what had become of me.

'Omi Daan.' Two words came out. I was surprised at how my voice croaked, like I was talking after a terribly long silence.

I realised I actually hadn't spoken much the past few days.

Neel's nostrils flared and his eyes narrowed. His fury seemed to be terrible. But it was not directed at me. I knew what he was thinking. I knew he was going to blame *him* for everything that had happened to me.

But what did Neel Sarathy know, I mocked. Something in me was shocked at how cold I felt towards my best friend. But the other part of me took over; I was not going to suffer any insult from Neel about *him*.

'I knew it,' Neel hissed. 'I knew it was him. What is wrong with you, Sonali? How can you let him affect you like this!'

My breathing quickened in anger and my eyes were filling, blurring Neel's tormented face.

'What are you talking about? What do *you* know about him?' I yelled.

He flinched at the spite in my voice and I regretted what I said the moment I spoke.

He composed himself and stood up straight, drawing himself to his full height. He was beautiful in a dangerous way when he was angry and I couldn't bear to look at him anymore. Instead, I turned my eyes towards Jo.

She had been sitting silently, her eyes were now probing mine. I knew why she didn't want to talk, knowing how her temper could get the better of her.

A calm Joanne. How weird, I thought. I could only imagine the storm that she hid inside.

I decided it was time to end their torment; they didn't deserve it.

'I'm in love with him,' I said. I wondered how a voice gone so cold could ever talk about love.

'We're not saying that you shouldn't be in love with him or anything, Li. Hell! We didn't even come here to talk about him. We came here for you, to find out why you're behaving like this. Tell me, did we do something wrong? Why are you so cold to us?' Jo asked softly, her voice barely above a whisper.

Neel looked like he was about to say something but Jo shook her head at him. He nodded stiffly and folded his arms across his chest.

'No. You didn't do anything,' I said after a long pause. 'I can't think of anything else. I see him everywhere I look.'

I saw their faces. They didn't understand what I meant.

'I see him everywhere,' I repeated. 'Literally.'

'You mean, even when he's not there?' Neel asked sharply.

'Yes.' I exhaled.

'How can you see him if he's not there?' Jo asked sceptically.

I had so many answers for that but none of them made sense. They didn't catch glimpses of Omi's sweet face smiling at them when they entered a room or heard Omi's voice calling out to them out of thin air. I wasn't suffering but it looked like I did. I wasn't happy either but my bliss was one I had never experienced before. I couldn't keep telling them something that they wouldn't believe. *It's all happening in your head*, that's what they would say. And I wasn't going to be forced to go to a shrink when nothing was wrong with my *head*. No one felt Omi's presence like I did because he chose me, and me alone, to *show* his presence. He could be miles away from me but I felt him there, right next to me.

They waited for me to answer. I looked up and shrugged. 'Yes. I just see him.' I nodded at Jo.

Neither of them looked convinced. Jo clicked her tongue and sighed. I knew what I sounded like: a troubled teenager who knew nothing of what she felt so strongly.

'You know that's not possible,' Neel said abruptly. He came closer to me and sat down on the bed, putting an arm around my shoulder. I didn't bother to shrug it off this time.

'How exactly do you see him? Like how you're seeing us right now?' Jo asked.

'Yah ... but not as clear. I see him suddenly when I enter my room; he's, like, smiling at me. The next second he's gone. And—and I hear him too ...' I fumbled, trying to explain in a way that didn't make me sound like I was mentally ill.

'Wait, you've spoken to him? Like, actually heard his voice?' Neel asked, tilting his head slightly.

I sighed. 'No. I have dreams about him. He talks to me there ... and so I know his voice.'

'You've never told us anything about that. So what? People get dreams; that's normal. No excuse for you to ignore us like this,' Jo said.

No! They couldn't get it! I looked at them helplessly. But I couldn't expect them to understand what *I* didn't understand either. They wouldn't leave me alone until they knew my problem; they wouldn't leave me alone even after they knew it.

'Tell us about the dreams,' Neel said, his voice cracking.

Omi wouldn't like this. He wanted *our* world to be intact.

However, it was Neel and Jo; I couldn't hold it back from them. And so I told them—the night I first saw him in the mysterious woods, the child who jumped from the bridge (I still didn't know why this was so crucial to me) and every night when I saw him, where we'd walk and talk and laugh together. I even told them about the road incident, one day before Neel's birthday.

'So that was like Omi and his sister? No wonder you were acting so strange,' Jo said. Her eyes narrowed and she nodded slowly, as if it was all dawning on her.

'This is—this is … different. I don't think you should talk to him anymore,' Neel said. His eyes were staring hard at the floor.

I gave a shrill humourless laugh. Neel had no idea of what he just said. Me stop talking to *Omi*?

Jo looked at me in shock; she couldn't take in the coldness that rippled from me.

'No, you have to stop,' Neel said firmly, his eyes still on the floor. He sighed and then looked at me. 'You and I both know that there's something absolutely wrong here! I can't find him on the whole of Facebook! I have looked for him everywhere online, I have tried to find him in the phonebook, in that school you named. And now! He's fucking your mind!'

'How dare you!' I shrieked. 'There is *nothing* wrong with him! I love him, I'm obsessed with him and it is *none* of your business!'

Neel didn't give up. 'It *is* my business, Sonali. Can't you see you're losing your mind?! Please let us help you, and please, stop talking to that mind fucker!'

I got up seething and pushed Neel so hard that he almost fell on the floor. Jo gasped in shock and called out my name. My body was shaking and my head felt like it was going to explode any moment. Neel caught my hand as I tried to bolt for the door; I couldn't stand another moment with them.

'Just leave me alone! Get out!' I yelled, yanking my hand free.

'Li! Calm down.' Jo caught my other hand.

Hot tears ran down my cheeks; I couldn't understand why I was reacting this way.

'Please, I need to be alone. Come back some other time,' I said through gritted teeth.

I couldn't look at their faces, masked with shock and hurt. I stormed towards the door and stood at the threshold, waiting for them to leave.

'Alright. We'll come again,' Jo said softly and walked out. She brushed my hands with her fingertips as she passed me and then she was gone.

Neel didn't say a word as he followed her. However, he paused when he reached me. He looked at me piercingly though I didn't dare to look back at him. And then he was gone too.

I slammed the door shut. I knew my sister would come inside any moment to find out what was going on, so I locked the door. *What have I done*, my mind kept asking. I sat down on my bed numbly. I clamped my hands over my mouth as I tried to fight back the hysterics that threatened to take over. My tears rolled down relentlessly and I collapsed on my back. I let the numbness take over; I succumbed to the emptiness that followed. I couldn't think anymore; I didn't want to.

The trees sway to and fro and the distant bird's song is fading. I can see the light ahead but I can't get there. I grope in the darkness, trying to get a sense of direction but the light only seems to get further away. I stumble forward, afraid that the light will forsake me. My eyes strain from focusing on the small throbbing light.

And then someone catches my hand. I stop short, trying to make out who it is. I can't see anything for a second but then, slowly, my eyes focus on a dark shape that stands tall, right next to me.

It is him! My heart beats faster in excitement. I gasp in wonder when I see him. He glows! His skin is pale and radiant; his eyes are shining and mirror the wonder in my eyes. His lips slowly curve in a breathtaking smile as he brushes his hand over my face. A slight breeze blows from behind me, rustling his boyish curls. He catches a strand of my hair that has blown across my face and tucks it behind my ear. I sigh at his perfection as he tilts his head towards me. And then he kisses me. My world melts away.

I am standing on a bridge. The rain is pouring down on my face and I can't see a thing. Déjà vu: I have been here before and something terrible has happened.

I freeze when I hear a sob. 'No!' I gasp and run towards him. He is holding the tiny doll in his arms again and staring at the dark waters below us. I can move this time; I am not going to let him fall!

I catch his hands firmly and shake him. He doesn't seem to feel my presence. His eyes never leave the raging water below. I call his name again and again, I try to lift his chin and make him face me; he just doesn't move.

I let go of him. My hands are aching from clinging to him and shaking him, my throat hurts from calling out his name. I slump on the ground, drenched and tired. My tears pour down my face along with the rain. I put my knees together, hugging them with my arms.

He regards me coldly and turns away. I close my eyes and sit there; it feels like forever. I hear him shuffle here and there, but he never leaves and I don't open my eyes.

Plonk! I close my ears with both my hands, trying to drown out the sound. He is gone. Again.

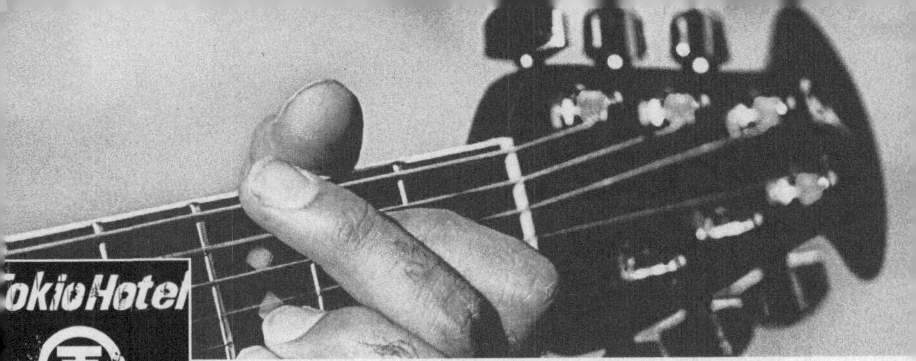

Neel Sarathy

I slammed my bedroom door shut, the sound echoing through the empty house. I kicked my Converse sneakers in a corner and turned the volume on the iPod speakers as high as it would go.

What the dang hell was wrong with that girl! Eight years of knowing her and being her best bud, and this was the first time I couldn't understand what was going on in her head. My mind kept replaying that moment when she almost pushed me off the bed. How absurd to act like that over a mere *guy*! The truth was, Li *never* did behave like that because of a guy and the way she got super pissed at me was truly scary.

Omi Daan, the mystery boyfriend. How could he have made her turn away from me and Jo just by chatting with her on Facebook? He hadn't even met her; it couldn't be 'love'. What was so damn attractive about staring at a computer screen for hours, chatting with a guy whom you haven't even seen in person?

No doubt the guy was hot in his profile picture but who knew? He could be faking it for all I knew.

I glanced at the clock that hung right above my bed, craning my neck to see. What a stupid place to have hung a clock where I couldn't even see it clearly from the bed. It was five minutes to six. Mum should be home any moment; at least she would get my mind off the crazy stuff that was going on lately.

Life sucked without that girl. I missed her silly remarks, singing with her crazily at the top of our voices whenever our favourite songs came on the radio, texting her, talking to her, hugging her … I wished she would just come to her senses and lose the guy for good.

My phone beeped. It was Jo.

Didn't really go well :p but don't worry. She'll come around. R u ok?

I sighed. What was she talking about it not having gone well; it downright sucked. I knew she was just trying to make me feel better; I hadn't even spoken a word to her after Li had kicked us out of her place. I texted her back:

Yeah I'm ok. Pissed as hell but I'm fine … wbu?

I waited for her reply but there was none, so I chucked the phone and plodded to the desk and switched on the computer. I opened the Facebook homepage and stared at it, feeling bizarrely creeped.

I guess our friendship was not worth what I thought it was to her. This was not the way we used to deal with things together; we used to confront each other if we felt things had gone wrong and then we would set them right.

The doorbell tinkled, announcing that Mum was home. I opened the door for her; she was dripping wet and carrying her ginormous handbag and another even larger and very full bag.

I took the bags from her. 'What happened? Why are you all wet?'

She shuffled inside, taking off her stilettos and placing them on the shoe rack.

'Car trouble. Had to take a bus home,' she wheezed.

'Do you know what was wrong with it?'

'I don't know, it wouldn't start. I thought I'd take an auto but I couldn't find one, so had to take a bus.'

'In this rain? You could've just asked someone for a lift, Mum,' I muttered, shaking my head disapprovingly.

'I know that, I just didn't want to impose on my employees.'

The window curtains were not drawn; I could see the rain pounding against the glass. Li loved the rain. I remembered that day when I had walked into her kitchen just in time to stop the tea from overflowing while she had been so busy looking outside and marvelling. She could get so easily distracted by small things that claimed her undivided attention.

'Hey! I'm talking to you.' Mum's voice cut through my reverie.

I glanced back at her. 'Huh?'

'How did your day go? Are you okay?' she scrunched her eyebrows worriedly.

'I'm ... good.' I shrugged and slumped down on the sofa.

'Hmm.' I knew she didn't buy it. 'Honey, I just walked in from the pissing rain and I don't think I can do a very good job trying to make you feel better. But you can tell me about anything that's bothering you. I'm right here.'

I snorted and she started laughing. My loving mother, always trying to have a laugh even at the worst.

'We went to see her today. It didn't turn out … too well. I just don't get her! She's, like, half-crazed over that guy and then she gets so mad at me when I try to tell her it's not at all good for her. I told her to stop talking to him and then she explodes! She's all, like, "just leave me alone" and "get out now"!'

My mum rubbed my shoulders and pulled me closer.

'Hey, hey baby. I thought things were getting better. I never expected her to say such things …' she began.

'No. She's—she's not in her right mind. I know her; this is not real …' Now why the hell was I trying to defend her?

'Okay. She's probably not in her right mind. But I don't want you hurting like this anymore.' Her tone was stern.

'Right. I'm not hurting, just not very happy,' I muttered.

'Listen. I have a surprise … You know I've been dying for a little vacation. So, I'm taking you somewhere for a week.' She beamed at me.

'Oh. And where will that be?' I asked dryly.

She frowned, not pleased with my level of interest. 'God's own country.' She winked at me.

What she talking about?

'Oh come on! I thought you were pretty smart.'

I rolled my eyes and sighed, 'Kerala.'

'Yes! Nice, na? You're going to love it!'

'Yah. Sure,' I said curtly.

'What's that? You've never been there before! Don't be

such a pessimist now. Tickets are booked for tomorrow night.' She waved her hand and disappeared to her room.

Great. Now I had to slog in some corner of the country for an entire week before I got back to the Li issue. But on the other hand, Mum was right; I seriously needed to get my mind off the craziness for a while. One week was not long enough to wreak more damage, was it? Nah, I needed a holiday and so did my mum. I was not gonna spoil the show with any more of my grubby behaviour. I was gonna chill my ass down in the clean and green of Kerala.

I called Jo to tell her I would be gone for a week. I was not gonna take my phone, 'cause the roaming charges would screw my allowance department. Jo pretended that she was absolutely thrilled for me but I could hear the anticipated loneliness that leaked through her voice. I felt kinda sorry for her, leaving her alone to deal with Sonali. But that's how things just were … and I couldn't help it.

After I hung up, I went through the call log. I looked at the number of times that I had tried to call Li. I felt tempted to try again, one last time before I left. I closed my eyes and wished that by some miracle she would pick up the phone. And then I hit 'call'. The phone rang and rang … and rang.

What the hell was I thinking? My fidgety hands were a sore pain to my heart. She was not gonna pick up her phone even if I wished on *all* the damn shooting stars. That was it!

When we finally were in the compartment—crowded platform, last-minute running, dog poop and pushing later—I claimed the topmost berth and buried myself for the rest of the evening. Mum went ahead and made the most of the opportunity of socialising with the good people around us.

It started to rain outside but our Green Express sped off. I plugged in my earphones and listened to music on my iPod. I closed my eyes and tried to visualise anything but *her.* Of course I only thought of her.

The funny part was I had never really missed Li the way I did now. It almost felt like I *needed* her, which I found strange.

Yes, she was the best friend I've ever had and of course I needed her but something about the way I'd started to yearn for her was unfamiliar. Memories of little things about her kept flashing in my mind. Like her hands; Li had the softest hands ever, they always made me envious.

And those eyes; Li didn't have very big eyes. There was a time in fifth standard when I called her Chinky; she'd almost punched me in the face.

I remembered the first time we'd all got drunk—Li, Jo and I. It was the summer after ninth standard. Li had almost kissed me, her eyes all narrowed and ... come to think of it, super seductive. I had neatly ducked and Li had landed up planting a big one on Jo's lips. We'd had a big laugh. But, right now, I was starting to think that it wouldn't have been all that bad.

And then I fell asleep on the first wave of drowsiness before I could unplug my ears. The next thing I knew, Mum was calling me down to have dinner. I quickly turned off the music, got down and settled in a seat near the window which my mum had kept for me.

I looked out of the window as I ate; lights flickered from the distance as the train sped away from the city limits. The glass was fogged and I couldn't see through it clearly. Though there was nothing much to see in the dark, I kept rubbing the glass and peering at the lights that flashed by. I plugged in my earphones again and listened to orchestral music. It was soothing and fitted perfectly with the rain and fog outside.

I kept staring at the glass window, now not bothering to wipe off the fog.

There was a face! The reflection was hazy, like smoke or a mirage. It was—it took me a moment to realise—*him*. I blinked and looked harder, sure that I wasn't seeing right. He stared back at me with an expression void of any emotion.

I turned back quickly to see if he was standing behind me. There was just my mum.

I looked back at the window. The face was still there. I could see more detail now. He was smiling, but there was no warmth. His jaws had hardened and there was something like defiance.

It couldn't be someone outside the train which was moving at such great speed. I looked around at the others, wondering if they could see him too but no one seemed to.

A tall lady caught my eyes, her eyebrows puckered in a question. I must've looked pretty shaken up. 'Are you okay?'

Mum turned towards me with a puzzled look on her face. 'What happened? Why is your face like that?'

'Uh ... Yes, I'm good.' I swallowed, peeking at the window through the corner of my eye.

The face was gone.

The others around us were starting to give me really weird looks. I figured it was time to bury my ass on top again.

I headed up to my berth and lay down.

I wondered if my head was really that messed up. *How* could I just see his face at a window?

That was it. Chapter closed. I had seen Omi Daan at the window of the train—I didn't know *how*—but I wasn't going to let it happen again. He had messed around with Sonali's head enough, I wasn't gonna give him a chance to mess with *my* head.

I realised, at eleven in the night, that it had been a stupid idea to leave my phone at home. I was bugged out of my mind. I was tired of trying *not* to think of the creepy window incident and I was frustrated that I couldn't fall asleep. I could've been texting Jo at least. Now I was pathetically stuck in this bunk, trying my best not to let my legs stick out over the edge.

After another hour of rolling left and right, I decided to visit the loo and maybe get some chill air so that I'd feel like snuggling back in my bunk and hopefully get some sleep.

I got down quietly and carefully. It was dark except for the lights near the two doors. After getting out of the AC compartment door, I saw that both the vestibule doors of the train were shut. Of course they were; it was midnight. What was I thinking? So much for chill air.

I tried the toilet door on my right. It was locked; someone was inside. I tried the one on the left. It was locked too. I sighed, propped myself against the wall and drummed my feet impatiently.

The people in the toilets were exceptionally quiet in the dead of night. I tried the doors again; they were definitely locked. This was starting to freak me out.

'Hello? Is anyone there?' I called out and tapped the door of the toilet on my right. No one answered. I tried the toilet on the left. I didn't get a reply.

I stepped back, wondering if I should just go back to my berth. Then the one of the doors shuddered. I looked at it cautiously, waiting for it to bang open and some dude to crawl out. Nothing happened. But someone was definitely inside and making weird sounds with the door.

I wasn't one of those brave souls who'd go knocking at a door that definitely didn't seem friendly. I stood there, ready to dash but also curious to see who would come out of the door.

But the doors never opened and I didn't have the nerve to try them again.

After standing there for what felt like hours, I went back to my berth. I crawled in, covered my body and my face with a blanket. Eventually, I fell asleep to even weirder dreams.

This trip just sucked so far.

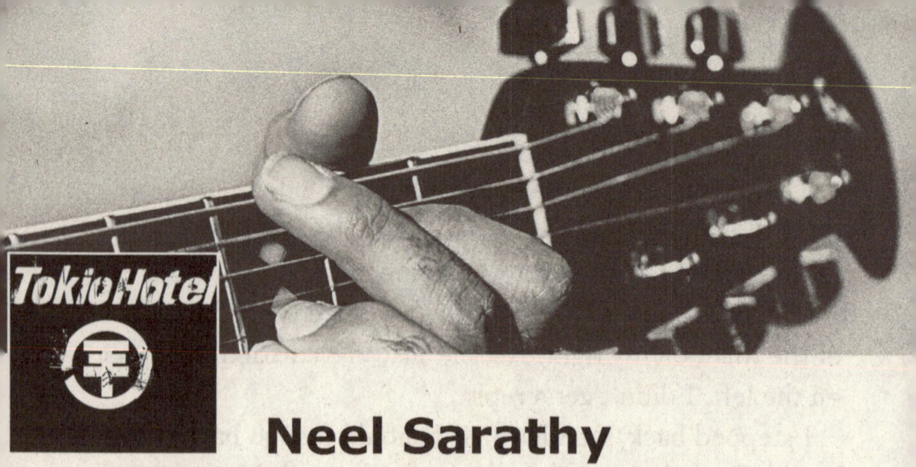

Neel Sarathy

I woke up chilled to my bones. I looked down and saw that everyone was still asleep. I checked the time on the iPod—5 am; four more hours till we reached Kochuveli, our destination.

I lay back down and closed my eyes to grab some more sleep. I couldn't help but think of what Li would be doing right now. Here I was, on a vacation and missing my best friends. Real pathetic. But the fact that I wasn't missed as much was hurting. Sonali. Her name rung in my head, sending a wave of panic and worry and longing.

A sudden tremor shook the train and I clutched the pole beside me. It died down quickly though.

The train shook furiously again; this time I was sure there was something really wrong.

'Mum?' I called out to her. She was sleeping in the middle berth just below me.

She stirred but rolled to her side and slept on. I looked at the others who slept as though nothing had happened.

I couldn't believe this. How come no one else felt the terrible shuddering of the train?

Again, like the previous night, I squeezed my eyes shut and forced myself to go back to sleep. I was not gonna get up until the rest of them had woken up.

Green. That was the only way to describe Kerala. I sat by the window and watched, mesmerised.

I fell in love with the bountifulness of the scene.

Suddenly, I realised that the tall lady from the previous night was talking to me. I raised my eyes reluctantly to her face and smiled tentatively.

'So how are you liking Kerala, beta? Your mom told me this is your first time here.'

'Yeah, this is our first time. It's beautiful.' I beamed at her. 'Is it your native place?'

'Yes, it is. But I live in Mumbai, so I visit once in a year.'

'Oh cool. I wish it was *my* native place too,' I muttered and looked out again, feasting my eyes on the landscape.

'Where will you be going?'

'Uh ... I'm not sure, Kochuveli for one.' It was so obvious; she laughed at me.

'I would have figured you were,' she said and laughed even more.

I glanced away as I did not want to have a long conversation with her. And what I saw made me wish I hadn't.

A tea vendor was passing by, with the usual steel tea vessel in his right hand, and a pack of tiny paper cups in the other. His voice rang out.

He was young, probably no older than me. And he was beautiful. His features were sharp and perfect; his hair was curly, and his eyes were almond shaped. Part of me wished he would look my way so that I could see what colour they were.

A pair of grey eyes bored into mine. At first, it was casual. But when he realised I couldn't take my eyes off him, his look turned to confusion.

His face. His eyes. So much like *him*. It was like *he* was standing right there, in person. My breath came out in short gasps.

He didn't move either. He stood there, rooted to the ground until someone called him, asking for tea. I couldn't even blink as he started towards me, wondering why he was heading in the wrong direction. I didn't realise it was Mum who had called him until she asked me if I wanted some tea. I snapped my head towards her.

'Neel, stop staring at the poor kid like that. It seems to be upsetting him and besides …' she stopped short, seeing the mortified look on my face.

'Are you feeling sick?'

'No, Ma.' My voice was barely a whisper.

'Then why is your face all white?'

The guy was in front of us. I looked up reluctantly. He smiled tentatively. His eyes were so warm and kind, so unlike the person he reminded me of. I blushed and looked away.

Mum followed my gaze and yelped when she saw the boy was closer than she had thought. Then she looked back at me, her eyebrows raised. This was so awkward! I wanted to go bury myself somewhere.

'Well … *chaikodu*?' Mum asked him in Kannada,

her eyebrows still raised. She looked amused; she was enjoying this.

He fumbled for the cups, filled a cup shakily and handed it to Mum, his head still down. I could see that he was biting his lip as if to keep himself from smiling.

Mum was purposely prolonging the moment by pretending the cup was too hot, taking a tissue and making a big fuss about holding the cup with it. There was a grin on her face as she asked him to give me one too. He nodded briskly and filled another one. I shook my head at Mum.

Our eyes met again as he handed me the cup. His gaze was so penetrating I had to force myself to concentrate on not spilling the tea. He smiled again and then turned to leave.

'Here's another one! And another … and another,' Mum squealed excited, running around the beach like a crazy little kid.

She was collecting seashells, something she had liked doing when she was a little girl. I couldn't help but smile fondly at her excitement. She was like a four-year-old. I gave her a thumbs-up sign.

I stopped drawing and simply looked at Mum. She was so happy. Without realising it, I teared up.

She walked up to me. The wind had picked up by now and her long skirt was flying around her.

'I told you not to wear a skirt,' I teased her as she sat beside me and gently laid the shells down.

'I told you it's comfortable and it's not a mini skirt, so that's not a problem.'

I grinned at her and got back to my sketching. It was turning out really well. All I had left to finish was some shading around the trees and in the sky. It was so exhilarating when you were drawing beautiful scenery which was right before your eyes.

'It's beautiful, Neel. Oh look! You even got me in it,' Mum beamed.

'Yes I did. Adds to the beauty, doesn't it?' I winked at her.

She laughed and put her arm around my shoulder. 'Want to tell me why you were crying?'

I sighed. 'It was just that … If Dad was with us right now, he would have been so happy too. And I was thinking how lucky I am to have you. I love you, Mum.' I put my head on her shoulder and she held me tightly.

'Oh baby, I know. It's still so hard without him, isn't it? But that's how it is. I love you and I'm lucky to have you too.'

We sat there for a long time, watching the sun set and the sea turn red. And then, as if my mind couldn't last a day without thinking about *her*, I wondered if she liked beaches.

I could imagine her sitting beside Mum and me (or minus Mum for that moment), being her dashing self with no Omi bullshit. She'd be laughing as usual; it was so easy to make her happy. Her slightly messy hair would be flapping around in all directions, which would annoy her after a few minutes, and she'd try to flip it back into place.

Two days in Kochuveli and I was already looking forward to leaving as we sat in the railway station, waiting for the train taking us to Ernakulam.

The two days had passed in a blur. We had wandered the beach, and every shopping spot, and had had three boat rides in the lagoon. Mum was ecstatic to be on water, which was weird to me. She later told me that the last time she had been anywhere near a water body was when she was sixteen, on a college trip to Goa. Phew! That must have been such a long withdrawal! And of course, our long indulgences in the restaurants; the food was amazing.

Back at the railway station, a lady announced in fluent Malayalam that the train had no plans of arriving for the next one hour. This small crumb of knowledge had been graciously imparted by one of the people patiently sitting next to us and waiting for the same train.

I looked around for something to distract myself with. Mum was already buried in the latest *Cosmopolitan*. I settled for trying to watch the action-filled, blood-spilling Schwarzenegger movie playing on the flat-screen on one of the pillars. I wondered if it was one of the *Terminator* movies; I wasn't an action-movie fan.

When the gore reached optimal level, I took my eyes off the screen. I looked at the guys sitting a few feet away from me. They were gawking at the flat-screen, clearly enjoying people blowing up into tiny pieces.

And then *he* walked right in front of me.

His hair was the first thing that caught my peripheral vision. Black, dark and rich, the kind that would make

Priyanka Chopra cry in a Sunsilk shampoo commercial. It was still as messy as the time I'd seen him on the train.

He paused. And as though he had actually felt my gaze, his eyes slowly travelled to me. When he caught my eye, he held it piercingly. A look of bewilderment and then delight and then bewilderment again crossed his face.

I got up, only one thing on my mind. I had to know who that boy was.

I walked up to him briskly, feeling my mum's stare boring into my back. I ignored the uneasy feeling in my stomach and kept walking towards him.

His expression was even funnier to watch. He took a step back, unsure of whether to walk away. He swallowed nervously but there was a glint of curiosity and excitement in his eyes.

When I realised that I hadn't been doing anything but staring at his face for the past few seconds, I cleared my throat and looked down at my shoes.

'Hi.'

I couldn't believe that actually came from him. He grinned widely.

'Hi,' I said meekly with a tiny wave of my hand, which probably looked kind of awkward.

'What's your name?'

'Umm ... Neel Sarathy.' I could not believe I'd almost forgotten my own name.

'I'm Daan,' he whispered.

No! I gasped. I shook my head tightly and looked up at him. Maybe it was just a coincidence that they shared the same name. This guy was real! Not some crazy shadow.

Panic filled me as I gazed into his eyes, looking for any assurance that he wasn't anything close to Omi Daan.

'Are you okay?' he asked me, his eyes filled with concern. No, this couldn't be Omi Daan.

'What's your full name?' I asked him, sounding sharp and menacing.

'Just Daan,' he replied curtly.

'I—I'm sorry, I didn't m-mean to be … rude,' I fumbled.

He nodded grimly and walked away without another glance.

I continued to stare at his back until he disappeared into a crowd of people. Before I started bawling or doing something even more stupid, Mum caught my hand and hauled me back to the bench where I had been sitting.

'Care to explain what just happened there?'

I looked at her warily. I didn't know how exactly I was going to tell her what had happened without bringing up the whole Omi thing, which would pretty much scare the hell out of her *or* she would decide I needed psychiatric help. I played dumb.

'Huh? Oh, I just thought of asking his name. You remember the *chaiwala* in the train?' I said coolly.

'Oh, the one you were flirting with? Of course I remember him.' She giggled, momentarily forgetting why she'd dragged me back.

'Yeah, that one.'

'So? Why did he walk off like that, leaving you with that mortified look on your face?'

I shrugged. 'Maybe he had somewhere to be.'

She went back to reading her magazine.

And quietly, I tried to figure out what could have made

Daan so upset when I asked his full name. Maybe it was just my panicked look? But he had looked concerned *before* I had asked his full name.

I was lost. Either being asked his full name was a big deal, which made no sense, or there was something more to this. I hoped he was just being obnoxious; the alternative was something I wanted to keep far away from.

The train finally arrived; an hour had never felt longer. We shuffled into the train, our luggage twice as heavy as it was when we started out from Bangalore. The train jerked forward and I fell asleep.

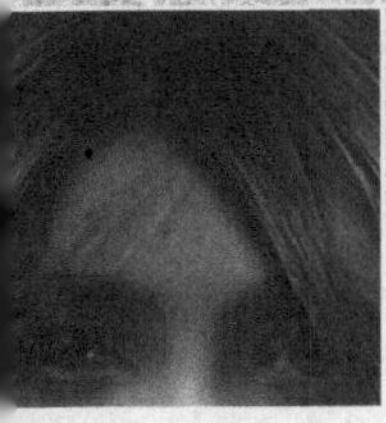

Sonali Machado

My eyes opened and fixed on the ceiling above me. I sucked in air rapidly; my lips were parched. A moment back, my eyes had seen terrible things, nameless fears and haunted dreams. I didn't know how I had escaped this time but I knew that soon I had to see *him* again. I feared him as much as I needed him. He could snap me to pieces with a finger but it was in his arms that I found my comfort. His voice rang in my ears when I was awake, when I was asleep.

His coldness cut through me like the sharpest blade even as his warmth filled me. I knew Omi Daan, every bit of his kindness and every shade of his darkness. He lived in me. He saw me through every day even when I had lost the people I loved. He spoke to me in a language no one could understand but the two of us. I lived halfway between our fantasy world and my insignificant reality. I laughed when he laughed. I shivered in cold and fear when he remembered the days he had needed comforting, when *he* was driven to madness.

My mother, my father, they didn't realise I had lost myself, even though I hardly to spoke to them. I greeted them in the morning and said goodnight before I went to bed at night. I was invisible to them most of the time and a small part of me would scream in panic inside my head, fearing that they didn't look at me anymore.

My sister was the only one left who seemed to care that I lived so dead. But it was her that Omi would force me to turn away from! I couldn't look at her longer than two seconds and she would sometimes yell at my rudeness. Or else, she would confront me with hurt and confusion in her eyes; that was the worst and Omi knew that it hurt me when she looked at me that way. He got angry and restless when I felt that way but promised me that he wouldn't hurt her if I stayed away from her. And so I did. And I lost her too.

I tried to get out of the house, get some air from the stale memories that piled up. I stepped out, dazed at the light that pierced my eyes as though I was emerging from a dark cell where I had been imprisoned. However, no sooner did I walk out on the road than I lost my way, my eyesight grew dim and I sank to the ground, my hands fumbling around me.

I vaguely remembered a helpful neighbour gently supporting me back to my house. My mother received me at the door, thanked the neighbour and took me back to my room. I gritted my teeth as tears trickled down my face. My mother asked me if I was not feeling well. I nodded feebly and she helped me back to bed, promising some medicine that would make me feel better. My sister watched quietly from behind her without saying a single word to me and then left when my mom did.

I clutched my pillow and buried my face in it. I sobbed uncontrollably, my head spinning from the images of pain and despair of another person's lifetime that filled me every second of *my* life. *Sonali*. He cooed my name; he was trying to comfort me.

Why?! I asked him, *why won't you let me free even for a while?* He chuckled at my pain, at my helplessness. He didn't answer. I waited for his response, trying to fight the wave of sleep that was washing over me. I forced my eyelids wide but they drooped and closed shut. He started humming a tune; he was lulling me to sleep. I gave up trying to fight it and sighed, hoping that he would end my torment for once and allow me a peaceful dreamless sleep.

And Omi Daan was kind that day; he let me sleep a deep sleep, his sweet voice at the background, still humming to me.

It was still light when I woke up. There was a bowl of soup on a tray on the table beside my bed. It looked cold. My mom must have put it there when I was asleep so that I could have something as soon as I woke up. I cupped a hand around my parched throat and then reached for the soup. It was still slightly warm and felt good to my throat. I swallowed slowly, letting the warmth slowly flow down.

How are you feeling? he whispered into my ears. He sounded happy for some reason and I smiled, pleased. He chuckled lightly and touched my hair with his finger. *I'm sorry*, he told me softly. I shook my head, wondering what he was apologising for. *Just drink now,* he said and I gladly went back to gulping the soup down, quenching my thirst.

I could feel him close for the rest of the evening. He seemed to sense my loneliness and would suddenly pull me to dreams where he would hug me warmly and sing to me. He didn't show me anymore of his painful past that night and I slept soundly again, like I had earlier in the day.

The next day was painfully different. Omi Daan was restless and wouldn't talk to me when I asked him what was wrong. He would suddenly burst with emotions and slap me with a memory that would almost break me. I was frightened of him and flinched from his voice when he tried to call me. This only made things worse.

Omi's whipping voice suddenly stopped. I slowly took down my hands from my ears where I had kept them almost throughout the day to keep out Omi's angry muttering and moaning. I sighed in relief but wondered warily what presence was here, strong enough to silence Omi.

My bedroom door creaked; a hand pushed it open.

And then she walked in. She had the same look of hurt and confusion that she had had the last time she had come. I sighed. I didn't know what to feel. My heart leaped in joy to see that sweet face but my mind knew better. I *feared* for her, feared that she had now drawn the wrath of Omi Daan upon herself as she hadn't before. She smiled at me slowly, afraid that I might snap at her any moment.

I looked at her full in the face. Her hair was shorter than I remembered; it hung just below her ears, straight and sleek. Her eyes were red and puffy as if she had been crying the entire day. They filled as soon as they met mine.

My heart was hammering in my chest and I looked around uneasily, tense at Omi's eerie silence.

'Li? Are you alright?' Jo asked me cautiously.

I snapped my head back at her.

'Jo!' I cried out and threw myself into her arms. She hugged me tightly. My breath came out in quick rasps and I sobbed helplessly. She rubbed my back and patted my hair.

'Sonali ... it's alright. I'm here now. What's wrong, Li? Tell me,' she whispered, holding me tighter.

I tried to find the words to answer but all I wanted was to tell her to run away as fast as she could. I could already feel the storm of Omi's anger building in the ominous silence.

Jo pulled back, she cupped my face gently but firmly with her hands and made me face her.

'You tell me, right now, what the hell is going on, Sonali. I am not going to leave you until you tell me *everything*. Do you know that I cried the whole day worrying about you and missing you?! I'm worried sick! And so is Neel, but he's not in Bangalore right now,' she told me.

I took a deep breath, shaking my head slowly and wishing she had not turned up. I met her gaze steadily and swallowed a lump that had formed in my throat.

'Jo, you have to get away from here right now,' I blurted out before I could change my mind and end up telling her too much.

She sucked her breath in shock and stepped back. Her tears started flowing. I forced myself not to reach out to her and instead stared at the floor so that she couldn't meet my eyes.

'No, I don't,' she snapped at me and grabbed my arm, slipping her hands into mine.

'You don't understand. You *have* to get out now or else … or else … he'll hurt you.'

I hoped I hadn't given away too much. Why couldn't she just leave! I couldn't bear to think of anything happening to Jo.

'Who? Who's gonna hurt me, Li? There's no one here except you and me. No one's gonna hurt me, honey.'

'No, you're wrong!' I took both her hands in mine. 'He's here, Jo. He's alive as much as you are! You can't see him but I do! I can feel him around me all the time and he doesn't like other people with me. Please understand! You have to go. Now.'

There. I had tried my best. She would leave now and Omi Daan would not do anything to her.

She looked at me like I had gone crazy. And then, her expression softened. She closed her eyes for a while as though she was concentrating on what she was going to say to me.

'You have to stop.' She opened her eyes and stared at me sternly.

'I can't, Jo,' I whispered helplessly. I knew that every second I spent with her I was bringing her closer to her doom but I missed her so much.

'What do you mean, you can't? What is he doing to you?' she whispered back.

A cold current ran through me, running deep through my bones and making me shiver. Jo shivered too.

'Did you feel that?' I asked her, my voice shaking.

She seemed too stunned to say anything. I knew she had felt it too. No! This could not be happening! Omi Daan had never manifested himself to someone else. Panic filled me. I *had* to get her out.

'Jo! Come, let's go …'

Before I could finish, my world disappeared.

I stand at the edge of a hill. My arms are clutched around my body and the wind whips at me, flailing my hair all over my face. I peek down and my knees shake at what I see. The hill slopes steeply down to a sinister-looking valley with a creek at the centre, chattering briskly.

I try to remember what happened a moment ago. I wasn't here; I was somewhere else, with someone else. I try to think harder. I was afraid of something—something that was going to happen. I just can't remember what it is.

Omi Daan. My eyes fly open. Yes! It has something to do with him! And then there is someone else too … I am missing something here, something so important that …

He pulled me away! What is he trying to hide from me? I have to know, now that someone else is involved. I have to stop him from doing harm to anyone else! What if it was someone I love? No …

'Omi Daan!' I scream, trying to get his attention away from whatever he is doing that he doesn't want me to know. No, he is not here. I can't feel his presence.

I try again. 'Omi Daan! Come here!'

No answer comes.

I take a step back from the edge. My knees are giving out

and I have to get far away from here lest I tumble down to a sure death. How long is he going to keep me here in the dark? I can't go anywhere. Heck! I know this place doesn't even exist for real; it is all in my head. This is just a memory … Omi's memory, not even mine …

Why?

I can't find the answer to that.

How? Because I am weak … Because I depend on him for everything: love, comfort and friendship. But I have all of that already. Yes, I had them all—my family, my friends … until he came along. It hurts to think of him this way; it feels wrong!

But I know it is the truth. I have to face it sooner or later. Omi Daan is like a drug, making me deteriorate every moment that I depend on him.

Right now, he isn't there with me and I am in total control of myself … But why can't I snap out of this darkness? How can he press me down in emptiness like this?

'Sonali.'

My mind freezes, so does my body.

No! It is he. He has come back to me. He will know exactly what I have been thinking about …

'Calm down, love,' he murmurs in my ear and slowly slides his arms around my waist. I flinch at his voice but I can't move.

'What did you do?' I ask abruptly.

He takes my hands and places them on his. His skin is warm and I feel good, as much as I fear him.

'What do you think I did?' he laughs.

'I don't know. Please! Tell me.'

'Don't you know?' he asks mockingly, nudging me gently back towards the edge.

I try to stand my ground but he is too strong.

'What are you doing?' I shriek, clutching him tighter.

'Why, Sonali? Why wouldn't you just trust me and only me? I promised you I wouldn't hurt you,' he whispers in my ear, his voice muted and harsh.

'Let go of me now!' I screech.

One foot is dangling in the air.

'If I do, you're going to fall! It's a long way down if you haven't noticed,' he laughs humourlessly but holds me back firmly.

'Omi!' I moan. 'Please!'

'Yes, darling. What is the matter? If I let you go, you're going to end up like your little friend.'

'What!' It was Jo! She was with me. What does he mean I will end up like her? 'What did you do to her?'

He laughs. 'I can't let anyone try to steal you away from me. I knew she was coming today but I didn't actually plan on finishing her like that. Aw! Come on now, don't be like that, love,' he croons.

'No...' I moan, struggling feebly to get his arms off me.

'It's going to be okay. I'm here now. I couldn't let you watch so I pulled you away. I brought you here.'

He runs his hand through my hair in an attempt to comfort me. I shake it off.

Get yourself together, I tell myself. I have to get back to reality; I have to see that Joanne is okay.

'Leave me alone!' I say through gritted teeth and then I push myself free, hurtling towards the dark creek below me.

I was face down on the floor. My legs were twisted at a funny angle and my hands fisted tightly. I heaved myself up slowly, relieved that I was not drowning somewhere in a dark creek. A sharp pain shot through my forehead. It was swollen slightly and I figured it was because of the fall. My vision was a bit hazy and I rubbed my eyes, trying to focus.

I was back in my room, safe. I had a weird feeling of hollowness. I clutched my heart waiting for Omi to cut through my thoughts as he had done every moment for the past few days but there was nothing.

I exhaled in relief. I couldn't believe what was happening. I was relieved and happy but lonely at the same time. There was a nagging thought that this was temporary and *he* was coming back. I shoved this thought away as quickly as it occurred.

My eyes slowly skimmed my surroundings. The bed was right beside me, inviting me to a deep untouched sleep where I could freely dream. No more tormenting nightmares and cold memories. I smiled briefly at that thought.

I caught sight of something else that lay on the other side of me, cold and lifeless.

It was Joanne Leslie. She stared at me through dead eyes. Her face was wet like she had cried to death and her arms stretched towards me, like the last thing she did was try to hold me.

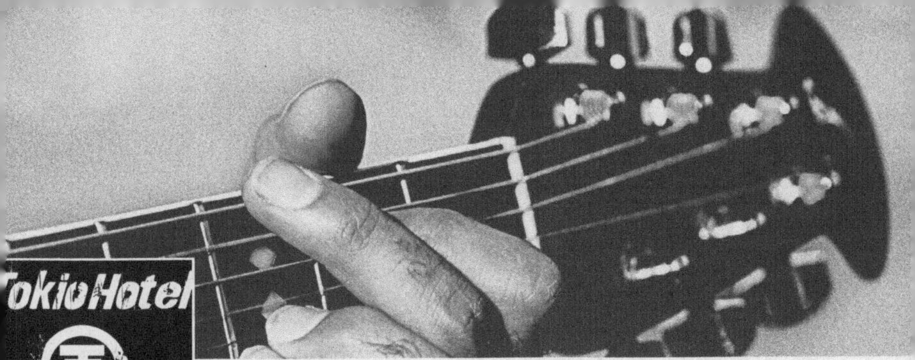

Neel Sarathy

'My, my! How wonderful of you to drop by.'

'What are you doing here?'

The guy is lounging on the couch like he owns the place and this is really ticking me off.

He laughs. Though I hate his guts, I can't help noticing how appealing and smooth it sounds.

I narrow my eyes. He has no right to be here and I have to make that clear.

'What? You trying to get all macho with me, huh? Face it, gay boy, you're no match for me,' he says menacingly. He kicks his legs off the couch and stands up.

'Get the fuck out of here, Omi Daan,' I hiss.

'Why should I? She wants me to stay with her. Right here.'

'You're using her! Just leave her alone, man,' I shout, bounding up like a crazy person.

I catch hold of his collar and shake him hard. Adrenaline pulses through me. I punch his face so hard that my hands go numb, but I don't care. It doesn't hurt. I push him back on the couch and aim one punch after another at him. A kind of madness fills me. He doesn't fight back, which is weird.

At one point, I regain my senses. I pull back, feeling him go limp on the couch. His head falls back and there is blood all over his face. I can't believe that I don't even feel sorry for him.

I stand up, wondering if I have killed him or something. But then, his eyes slowly open. He lifts his head and looks at me. He doesn't look angry or hurt or anything. He just stares at me blankly and his face suddenly blurs and it is Daan who is looking at me.

I gasp in shock, trying to make sense of what just happened. He lifts a hand, beckoning me to come closer to him.

'It's you again! Why won't you leave me alone?' I shriek, jabbing a finger at him.

And then his face contorts grotesquely. Omi Daan's cocky face looks up at me, clean and unblemished.

'That was close.' He winks at me, crossing one leg over the other.

'Damn you! Whatever the hell you are, I want you to leave Sonali and me alone, do you understand?'

'Well, Sonali and I can't live without each other so we have to get rid of anything that comes in our way. Do you realise what a pain in the ass you've been all this time? She's sick of you! Why don't you just leave her alone to her happiness?'

'Her happiness?' I shriek again. 'Listen, I'm ordering you to leave her alone!'

He purses his lips and closes his eyes, as if deep in thought. I want to punch a hole through his head for being so calm and indifferent.

'Hmm … I'm afraid that's not possible, Neel.' He shakes his head and opens his eyes wide.

'You will leave her alone.' I bend down and hiss at his face.

'Then I'll just have to take you down as well. Although, it'll be even harder for her to lose both of you.'

He lunges at my throat with his hands.

'Neel! Neel, wake up! What are you doing?'

I heard her screaming but I couldn't open my eyes. Something was strangling my throat but I couldn't get it off, I couldn't find my hands. What was the matter with Mum? Couldn't she just get it off me?

What are you *doing*?

Then I felt it. My own hands were clutching my throat. I was strangling myself!

My eyes flew open. Mum was frantically trying to pry my hands off my throat. I coughed, trying to get some air in. But it was no use; my hands weren't slackening their grip. I was going to pass out any moment.

'Neel! Neel? Listen to me, baby.' Mum's voice seemed far away.

Someone was slapping my cheeks. I was slowly slipping … I could breathe. I coughed up hard and inhaled as much air as I could. My hands were no longer at my throat.

I looked up at Mum. She was wiping the sweat off my face and whispering that everything was okay.

Behind her, every pair of eyes in the compartment was fixed on me.

Mum hugged me tightly. 'What was *that* about?' she whispered in my ear.

'I don't know, Mum. Honestly,' I whispered back, wishing that those people would stop gaping at us.

She nodded and looked back at the people. 'Alright! Everything's okay now. Sorry for the commotion, people,' she said, managing a weak smile.

Some of them nodded and turned away politely while most of them continued to gawk at us.

'I'm so sorry, but I can explain,' I told her shakily.

'Yes, you most definitely will explain to me why you tried to strangle yourself,' she retorted, keeping her voice down.

I sighed. This was so not going to be easy. I guess I'd need to tell her everything from the start to make her believe me.

And then it hit me. I sat back heavily.

Then I'll just have to take you down as well. Although, it'll be even harder for her to lose both of you.

What did that mean? Lose *both* of us?

'Mum! I need your phone!' I grabbed it from her hand.

She stared at me open-mouthed.

I punched in the only phone number I had ever bothered to memorise.

'Hello? Li! Are you okay?' I exhaled. I was relieved that she had picked up her phone at last, though some intuition told me something was terribly wrong.

'Neel? It's Li's mother ...'

I cut her off. 'Is she okay?'

'No, Neel. She's not okay. Joanne died this evening. She came over to see her and we found her dead in Li's room.

Where are you? Sonali needs you, Neel. She's in shock,' she sobbed at the other end.

I sucked in some air. Jo was dead. My tears trickled down before I even knew.

'Yes, aunty. I'm coming back. Tell Li—tell her that I'm on my way. I'm still in Kerala but I will be back by tomorrow.'

'What happened? What do you mean you'll be back by tomorrow?' Mum shot out, plucking the phone out of my numb hands.

'Jo died. Li needs me.'

'Wha–what? How? Are you sure?'

I clutched my face with my hands and sobbed, shaking furiously. I wished I had not taken this stupid trip but stayed there instead. I could've been with her, I could've even stopped whatever it was that had happened to her!

And then I knew. It had to be *him*! That was what he had been telling me in the dream. Rage boiled through my veins. I *had* to get to Sonali. I *had* to stop him from hurting her or me or anybody else he planned on *getting rid of.*

'Mum. We have to go back today. We have to go back to Bangalore,' I said, clutching her arm tightly.

She was crying quietly. Jo was dear to her as well. Jo was dear to all of us.

'Neel, I'm so sorry about Joanne. We'll catch the first train going to Bangalore as soon as we reach Kochi, okay?' she said.

We found a train back to Bangalore soon after we reached Kochi. Mum hastily bought two non-reserved second-class tickets. After loading ourselves into the train and hoping that no one with reserved tickets would come to claim our seats, we sat down and waited for the train to move.

We didn't say a word even as the train started back towards Bangalore. It was a long night; I couldn't get a wink of sleep.

Thoughts ran wildly in my head. I wondered if Li would still in be in love with Omi even after knowing that he was responsible for Jo's death. I remembered how she'd been sickeningly into him the last time I saw her. It made me almost ... jealous.

Almost immediately, I remembered that Jo was dead and here I was wondering if I was *jealous* of someone. It seemed like only yesterday when we'd both gone over to Li's place, fought over paying the auto guy and comforted each other after what had happened with Li.

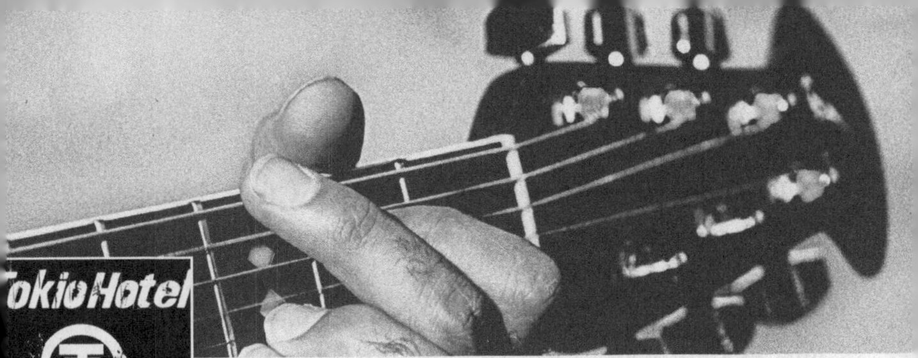

Tokio Hotel

Neel Sarathy

Li's dad met me at the door.

'Neel,' he said, sounding relieved at seeing me.

'Uncle,' I greeted him with a weak smile.

'Come inside, come inside.'

'Where is she, uncle?'

'She's in her room,' he replied heavily.

I took a deep breath. And then I walked towards her too-familiar room, which I hadn't seen in a long time.

The door was slightly ajar and I could hear Sonya's voice faintly. I couldn't really make out what she was saying. I nudged open the door gently, not wanting to startle them. And then I saw her.

She was sitting on the bed, her legs folded and her hands limp on her lap. She was looking straight at me when I caught her eyes and I held them steadily.

I yearned to let her know that everything was going to be okay. Her eyes had something so different in them that I couldn't make out at first. I looked closer and I saw that it was pain.

I crossed the distance between us swifter than I had ever moved and before I knew it, I was holding her in my arms. This was it. This was all the assurance I needed that we were going to get through this *together*. She held me just as tightly and I was so happy that she was responding to me after ages.

'I've missed you,' I told her when I could breathe at last.

She didn't answer, but she pressed her cheeks closer to mine and her body shook with sobs.

'Hey, I'm right here now. Everything's gonna be alright,' I whispered in her ear.

I didn't notice when Sonya had left the room but when I looked around, I saw that we were alone.

She cried and I sat there and held her as long as she wanted me to.

When the sobs died down, I looked into her face.

'Li, I need to ask you something.'

She sniffed and nodded at me to go on. I made her look me in the eye. Her eyes were puffy and red but they were still Sonali's. And they were beautiful.

'How did it happen? It was *him*, wasn't it? What did he do, Li?'

And then she told me everything. From when she had started seeing him in her dreams until the time when she had found Joanne lying still after he had pulled her into a dream. The dream-pulling part truly frightened me. I was horrified when she told me he could do that to her whenever he wished. But, of course, not anymore.

'He's gone now?' My voice came out in hoarse whisper.

'Yes. I don't know exactly how but I think I shut him out

now. I think it was the shock of Jo's death.' Her eyes were sparkling with tears.

I exhaled in relief; at least he wasn't a threat to her right now.

'Do you think he's gone? Like forever? Do you think he's coming back?' Her voice started rising in panic.

I reached out for her hand and squeezed it tightly. 'I don't think he's really gone.'

I told her everything that had happened from the time I had left for Kerala. I even told her about Daan. She was too stunned to speak but she listened attentively.

We sat there in silence for a long time. She furrowed her eyebrows and stared hard at the floor like she was deep in thought. I had done my quota of thinking all of last night and this morning. I could feel sleep weighing me down but I tried my best not to let my eyelids droop.

She noticed. 'Neel, you look so tired! Have you not slept?'

'Oh. Um … not really.' I shrugged, not wanting to make a big deal of it.

'You didn't get a wink of sleep last night, did you?'

When I didn't reply, she sighed. 'Hey, why don't you go home and rest, for now? I'll see you in the evening. You look like you're going to pass out any moment, Neel.'

She got off the bed and tried to pull me up.

I grabbed her arm and made her sit down. 'No, I'm not going yet. I can't leave you alone, Li. We need to do something about this. How can I know that you're safe, huh? How will I know he's not gonna hurt you.'

'He can't get to me anymore, Neel. But he can still get to you, seeing that he tried to kill you. How can you sleep if he gets to you through your dreams? I'm so sorry that I brought this upon you and Jo! It's all my fault and now I can't even stop him from getting to you. Oh my god, Neel. What are we gonna do?'

She did bring it upon us by talking to Omi *freaking* Daan and then actually falling for him. I bit back the rage that almost exploded from my mouth.

But this wasn't her fault. She didn't know that he was going to turn out to be this psychopath who we were not even sure really existed.

'No, it's not your fault. We're gonna get through this together. No matter what ...' I couldn't finish. I stifled a yawn.

'Just sleep here, since you're so determined to protect me. You might even be safer. Want me to call your mom?'

'Yeah, okay,' I mumbled, already making myself comfortable on her bed.

I closed my eyes and before I knew it, I drifted into the deepest sleep I'd ever had, making up for a sleepless night and not to mention the two waking days that went with it.

When I woke up, I knew it was late.

I sat up. My head gave a little spin and I looked up at the clock, disoriented.

It was 6 pm. I had come to Li's place at around eleven in the morning. I rubbed my eyes and my face, hoping I hadn't drooled all over my face or done anything embarrassing like that.

The door clicked open. It was Li.

'Oh, you're awake.' She smiled at me warmly.

It was so good to see that smile when I had spent the last few days thinking that I would never see it again.

'I'm sorry for napping for so long. I hope I didn't cause any trouble,' I said absentmindedly, getting up and going towards the bathroom.

'Yeah, right. You sleeping and breathing and lying still over here caused the greatest havoc ever witnessed at home,' she snorted, rolling her eyes.

It was good that the girl had got back her sense of humour. However, our little stolen moment of laughter was only a shadow of what laughter used to be. An image of Joanne grinning at a silly joke flashed through my mind. I could see that Li was going through the same anguish as she turned her head away, lips quivering.

'I had the most peaceful sleep I've had in weeks,' I told her. 'Must have had something to do with sleeping on your bed,' I added cheesily and winked at her.

'What, you're decided to be straight now?' she snorted and laughed.

I opened my mouth to give a smart-ass reply but stopped short. I looked at her and frowned. Did she really mean what she said or was she just falling back to her familiar pattern of teasing me? For once, this felt different. Or maybe it was just *me* who felt different.

'Can I tell you something?' I asked, looking at her straight in the eyes. I walked up to her and sat down on the bed.

She stopped grinning, sensing that I was going to say something serious. 'Sure. What is it?' she asked, concerned. Probably thought it was something about Omi again.

'I might just be in love with you,' I said and smiled.

There, I had said it. Gay boy just professed his love for the girl who had always meant the most to him.

How had I not realised before? When I looked into her eyes and felt loved and secure, I'd been in love with her. When I felt so much joy when she had hugged me or held my hand, I'd been in love with her. Even when I had gone crazy about the many boys I had liked and then un-liked, I'd always been in love with her. I couldn't let her slip away anymore. She had to know it now. And forever.

The first expression was disbelief and shock. This slowly softened—I couldn't quite make out what it was.

I waited for her to say something. She swallowed and then grinned at me. Something about that look she gave me kind of made me feel like I was going to melt. And then suddenly, before she could say anything, she passed out in my arms.

'Li! Li? What the … Listen to me, Li! Are you there?' I shook her as hard as I could but she was limp. I lay her on the bed.

Her mum, dad and sister came rushing into the room.

'What is it? What happened to her?' Her dad shook her, almost knocking me off the bed.

'I don't know. She just fainted! Is she on medication or something?' I asked, taking Li's hand and rubbing it, trying to get her warm.

'No, she's just been taking some Paracetamol for her headache,' her mum said, running her hand over Li's forehead. 'She doesn't have a temperature. Sonya, get some water. Quick. And Neel, are you sure nothing happened to her?'

'We were just talking and she passed out.'

I couldn't bear to think of the possibilities of *why* she had passed out and what exactly could be going on inside her head.

'We have to get her to wake up!' I shrieked in panic, shaking Li again.

I couldn't let her go through this any longer. Who knows what he could be doing to her? I had just survived his attempt to kill me in the train yesterday. And we had been having our most intimate conversation ever …

I had to stop him.

I had to get in there myself. I had to get into *her* dream.

I had no clue how I was going to do that. I couldn't fall asleep for the next two days in sheer tension. I knew I had to fall unconscious or something to get into the other realm.

I had to try another way: get hit and pass out. If I asked her dad to punch me in the face right now, they'd probably send me to a mental hospital.

Think, I told myself.

I looked around desperately, searching for something that might help me become unconscious.

The whitewashed blank wall to the right of Li's bed. There was some free space in front where I could run for more impact.

Sonya and her mum were splashing water on Li, slapping her face and trying hard to wake her up.

I walked up to the right of the bed. They didn't even notice me move until I stood facing the wall, trying to judge the force of the impact I could get with the very short distance I could run.

'Neel? What are you trying to do, son?' Li's dad asked me cautiously.

I didn't reply. I could probably break my skull with what I was about to do.

I ran smack against the wall. For a moment, the pain was so sharp that it felt like all the bones in my skull had cracked. And then I blacked out.

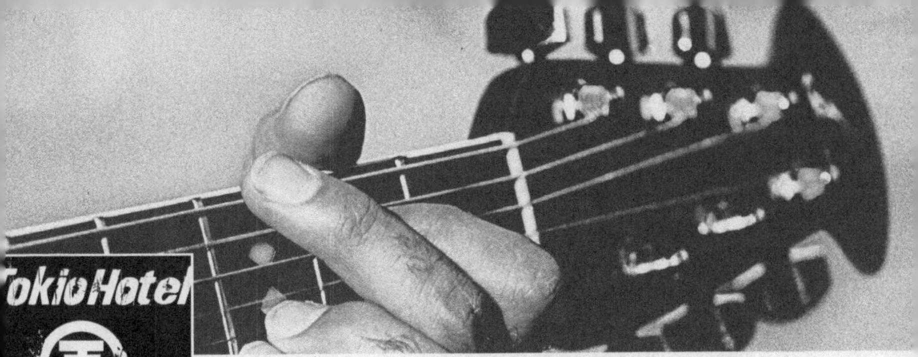

Neel Sarathy

Everything is dark. I can't see, can't hear, can't breathe, which is weird because I am not suffocating either. I just can't feel anything. I am a void and everything around me is a void.

I just lie there … I can't remember what brought me here or how I got here or … wait. Who am I?

I can't remember that either. I laugh, though I can't feel where the sound is coming from or where the sound is going. Am I dead?

Probably not.

Then *what* am I?

A ghost? Again, I have to be dead to be a ghost. Wait. Something about 'ghost' reminds of … come on! Think harder.

Yes! I can remember something … pain!

There is something I want to do, I *have* to do! What is it?

Neel.

That is my name. I think harder. There is someone else involved here.

Sonali.

Memory rushes back, making me dizzy. Everything that she said comes back to me, her voice playing in my head. I remember my brilliant plan of head-smacking the wall and almost killing myself. Did it work? Where am I?

I have to concentrate now.

And then, somehow, I open my eyes. It is weird because at first, it feels like I don't have eyes, or a body for that matter. And then, suddenly, I am squinting and trying to see through a really bright light, which almost blinds me. Now where does all that come from?

Focus, Neel.

I pull myself up. I look around. I am in a forest or woods or ... There is no one else around me but something tells me I have to search. I can feel that Li was around here, somewhere.

I haul myself to my feet and sway a bit, almost losing my balance. And then I start running. I don't even know where my feet are leading me but I have this feeling that my instincts are all I need to trust right now. The trees pass by in a blur and I am surprised that I don't get hit by any. I am not a very good runner but somehow, I don't lose momentum.

I stop. I stand panting, clutching my stomach and try to catch my breath.

Someone is watching me from behind. I snap around. Nothing.

Something stirs towards my right.

At last. I have found them.

I falter. My knees feel weak. He is kissing her. Like really really *kissing* her and she seems to like it. He has one hand on her waist and the other is caressing her neck.

I am so mad I want to snap his pretty neck into two. Maybe I can.

I lunge forward, an ugly snarl building up in my throat.

He looks up at me lazily as I charge towards him, a triumphant look in his eyes. The next moment, I knock him aside and we are both flat on the ground.

I hear her yelp in shock as I wrestle Omi, trying to punch every part of his face. He laughs sarcastically, taking my blows and not even trying to protect himself.

'Neel! What are you doing?' she cries, trying to pull me back.

I want to shout at her to get back because I am planning on thrashing Omi and she could get hurt. She tries to lock my arms with her hands. Why is she trying to stop me?

I let go of Omi, get up and glare at her.

'What were you doing with him? What's wrong with you?' I shake her.

'What do you mean? I was just—I was just ...' she can't finish.

Her eyes flick towards Omi who is sprawled on the ground. She narrows her eyes, like she is confused at what she is seeing. And then she looks back at me.

'I have no idea what just happened,' she says and seems truly frightened.

'What? Are you serious?' I look closely at her. She is telling the truth, I can see.

'Oh my god, you really don't know what happened. You do know this is a dream, right? You passed out when we were talking in your room and I kinda followed you.'

'Followed me? How?'

'I banged myself on your wall to knock myself out and here I am.'

She grimaces. 'Why is he bleeding on the ground?'

I look menacingly at him. The guy isn't as strong as he seems.

The next moment, he is not there.

Instinctively, I pull Li into a tight grip.

'Neel! We have to get out of here! He's gonna come for us,' Li shrieks, pulling me along and running.

I follow her without a word. Only thing, I am worried if there is a way out. This is a damn nightmare after all, and I suspect it is completely under Omi's control.

'And yeah, you were making out with him,' I say accusingly as we sprint, holding hands.

'Shut up,' she says, not believing me and takes a sudden turn, making me almost run smack against a pine tree.

'What! I'm not lying. But good you don't remember.'

I pick up speed and run in front of her. I have to yank back her hand which nearly slips from my grip.

'Hey! I really don't see the point of running though,' I say. I slow down and pull her to a halt as she skids past me. She throws her arms around me, panting.

'Easy, easy,' I tell her, patting her back.

'No, there is a point,' she says between breaths. 'I don't like that place. I feel like I've been there for a long time but I can't remember anything.'

'Not good.'

She frowns. 'We were making out? I hate him! Neel, we need to find a way out of here.'

'I know. We will.'

'Just don't wake up before I do, please. He's gonna kill me.'

'No. We're gonna end this now, once and for all. We need to face him and *make* him leave us the hell alone, yeah?' I say, my voice sounding hard and resolute.

She nods her head furiously and tries to hide the trepidation that I can see so clearly in her eyes.

'Now take a deep breath and close your eyes,' I tell her and gently press her eyelids shut with my fingers.

She takes a deep breath and exhales slowly.

'Now concentrate and try to find out where Omi Daan is. If he's here right now, tell him to show himself to us.'

For a long time, she doesn't say anything. Her eyes are still closed and she squeezes them tighter like she is concentrating very hard on something. A bead of sweat breaks out on her forehead. I wipe it away. Her head is already clammy from running.

At last, she opens her eyes, which look faraway and vacant. 'He's here.'

'Where?' I look around.

'Behind you,' she whispers.

Before I can turn, he whispers in my other ear. 'Hello.'

When I turn, Omi is a few feet away from me.

'Tell me—what exactly is your brilliant plan to make me leave you alone?' he asks scathingly. He leans lazily against a tree and folds his arms.

'What do you want? What are you?' I ask the first things that come to mind.

'Those are simple questions.' He shrugs. 'Don't hold my girl's hand while I'm answering.'

'She's not your girl!' I snap, holding Li tighter.

He is in my face, his nose nearly touching mine. His eyes are blazing dangerously. 'You fucking do what I ask you.'

I think he is going to throw me down and break all my bones. But he doesn't. I wonder if he *can't*.

'Wait! You can't touch me, can you?'

He takes a step back. I think I see fear behind his nonchalant expression. *He* can't touch *me*. He straightens his back, and turns to Li.

'I love you,' he tells her clear and loud. His voice has a ring of sincerity.

'Don't you dare!' I yell and sprint up to him, knocking him so hard that I could have broken a knuckle.

This time, he fights back. In a while, he has me pinned against the tree he was leaning on.

'You can't kill me, you idiot!' he laughs. 'I'm already dead.'

I kind of know that but it is still a big shock to find out that I am fighting a dead guy. Something connects in my head; Li's dreams somehow make sense now. The kid who fell off the bridge in her dream must be *him*.

Li stands rooted to the ground. Her hands are fisted into balls and she is shivering. Her eyes are on us. I don't know if she is looking at me or him.

I blurt out before I can stop myself, 'You jumped off a bridge?'

'She told you.' He glares at me after throwing an accusing look at Li.

He walks over to her lithely and pulls her into a too-tight embrace.

'You know she doesn't really give a damn about you.' I stagger to my feet. 'Why are you still hypnotising her? What do you want from her? A sister, since you lost yours? A girlfriend, since you're dead and never had one? Can't you just let her *live*?'

There is a dead look in Li's face and her eyes are fixed on Omi like she is under the influence of a very strong love potion.

Omi pulls her closer as I speak. He buries his face in her hair and inhales deeply. 'I want her and everything that comes along with her.'

He laughs spitefully. I can almost feel the acid in the air.

'I *am* in love with her,' he says solemnly. His look is so vulnerable and soft that I almost believe him.

But he wouldn't hold her captive like this if he really loved her as he said he did.

'Which is complete bullshit,' I snicker.

Li isn't in his arms anymore. She is gone. I blink twice to make sure that I am seeing right. She isn't there.

'Where is she?' I cry. Panic fills me. I haven't followed her all the way here just to lose her again. I have to know that she is alright. 'Do you know where she is?'

'She's awake now.' He shrugs. 'Now I'm guessing you want to get back too?' he says, as if he was relieved that we are all happily saying goodbye.

'No. I want to get this over with and I want you to leave Sonali alone. And what you did to Joanne. Unspeakable,' I say, trying not to choke.

A nasty smirk plasters his face.

'I could say I'm sorry about her but I'm not, so I won't waste my breath,' he says callously, as if Jo is a rag he tossed away.

'Like you have any breath left in you. You're dead. Accept

that and move on. You didn't have to take her life; you didn't have to destroy her. She didn't do anything to you.' My voice comes out flat and cold.

'She was distracting Sonali from me,' he says. 'And I couldn't let that happen. You need to go now.'

Everything is a haze as soon as he says those words. My vision blurs and everything around me seems part of a spiralling mist. His face dissolves. I want to know what he is trying to do to me now, but I can't see anymore. And then suddenly, my mind feels like it has been freed from my body. My soul is flying.

I wait for the flying and the paralysed feeling to fade. And then everything is quiet for a while, until I hear someone call my name. I try to ignore the uncomfortable numbness that is slowly spreading from the back of my head, engulfing my forehead and thumping on my temples.

The voice was persistent.

When at last I decided to pay heed to it, it exploded in my ears. The numb feeling was replaced by a sharp, throbbing pain. My head felt like it had been split in half. Somehow, I forced myself to open my eyes.

I wanted to clamp my hands on her mouth before she could yell my head off; she was calling out my name as if we were worlds apart and her mouth was right next to my ear. Apparently, she was trying to wake me up but I wouldn't be surprised if I became unconscious again. The girl could really scream!

I tried to open my mouth and tell her that I was okay

but all I could do was twitch my lips weakly, making an incoherent sound. I tried to lift my hands but they felt awfully heavy. Damn! Did I really screw myself up so badly?

By now, she had realised I was awake and had stopped screeching into my ear, which was a relief. Someone was dabbing my head with something cool which kind of eased the throb in my head. My vision was still blurred so I could only make out a vague shape that looked like Li bending over me, telling me that everything was okay. Her voice seemed far away now, maybe because it was softer.

I tried to say something again, like ask why everyone was fussing over me. Okay, maybe I had wall-slammed myself but here I was, awake and feeling very out of shape but still fine enough to know what was going on around me. I vaguely noticed another shape looming over me and gently nudging Li aside.

Damn! Why was it taking so long for my vision to get right?

The strange shape didn't look like anyone from Li's family. It was a man, I could tell, a plump little man. He was examining my head and I could feel where his cool hands touched my face, tilting it from one side to another. He was saying something which was, again, too far away for me to hear. I so badly wanted to get my darn senses back and know what the hell was going on. I knew that head injuries could dull your senses for a while, but how long did it usually last? Not too long, I hoped. I still had so much to do about Omi and right now, I desperately needed to talk to Li.

And then the thought struck me. What if I was gonna be stuck like this forever? It could happen, right? I'd seen a movie where this figure-skater girl had a nasty fall and became blind forever. She could only make out bright lights and vague shapes, kind of like I could right now. Oh my god! Panic filled me. I didn't want to go blind, or deaf or paralysed. What had I done to myself!

Calm down, Neel—I tried to collect myself.

Calm *freaking* down?! The majority of my mind screamed at the calm part. I could possibly be turning into a vegetable now! I didn't need to calm down. I needed to shock myself into full consciousness.

A sharp stab of pain poked my left wrist. I wondered if one of those great ants with their huge stinger-butts had had a piece of me while no one was looking. And then, ironically, after my plans of shocking myself awake, I slowly drifted. A kind of numb ease spread over my body, replacing the numb uncomfortable feeling.

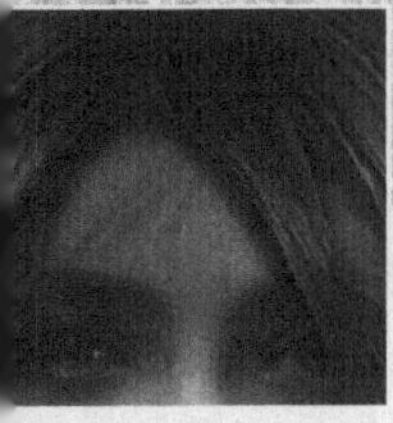

Sonali Machado

He had been knocked out for two days. The doctor said that he needed to rest. There was no knowing if his senses were going to come back to him until he woke up from his coma-like sleep. And so he couldn't be there at Jo's funeral.

I had been too numb to register much of what happened at the funeral. I only remember that she'd been dressed in a regal purple gown covering her to her toes. It would have pissed her off real bad if someone had ever dared to try to dress her like that when she was alive. This thought had made me hysterically giggle and then sob, making people throw wary glances in my direction.

I was getting accusing glances anyway. Everyone knew that Jo had died when she came to see me after I had been acting funny for a couple of weeks. Even Godzilla, who had given her so much grief a few weeks back, glared at me. How long ago it all seemed!

The burial was the hardest.

Wind and rain whipped us as we stood around the grave where Jo's coffin was lowered into the muddy hole already half filled with water.

The coffin sank into the grave. I bit my lip to stop the agonised moan that was building in my throat. Blood trickled down my lips, and was quickly washed away by the rain.

The oversized thorns on the rose I was holding had broken my skin. But the pain was soothing. The moment I dropped it down into the watery grave, I felt a hollowness so dense that it seemed that the soul within me had fled from my miserable body.

And all through, I was almost insane with worry over what must be happening with Neel.

I remembered Neel telling me that he 'might just be in love with me'. That moment could have been so beautiful, until *he* interfered. I cried harder, gritting my teeth in anger and regret.

'Sonali?'

Ma peeked into my room, her small silver phone in her hand.

'What is it?' I asked, quickly brushing off the tears from my face.

There was a warm smile on her face, something I had not seen for many days. I looked at the phone in her hand and sucked in my breath.

'He's woken up?'

She nodded her head slowly. 'Yes.'

'Oh my god! Can I go? Please?'

I got up before she could say anything. As I was washing my face, I heard her say 'sure' and something about Dad dropping me to the hospital. All I could think of was seeing Neel again. I wanted to tell him how much I'd missed him and that I was so sorry for what had happened to him.

Santosh Hospital was not far from my place. A couple of minutes and we were there. Sonya was there too. She took my hand as we stepped out of the car.

I knew the room number 'cause I'd been there the entire first night. Neel's mom had asked me why he had run into a wall. I hadn't known what to tell her. Playing dumb was not easy. All our parents were wound up after Jo's death.

The door was closed but we could hear someone laughing. It was Neel's mom. I sighed in relief.

'Li! You're here!' he threw his arms wide and grinned at me.

I stopped short for a second, staring at him. He was sitting up in bed, propped against a pillow.

I grinned back at him. 'Of course I'm here.'

And then I walked into his arms as fast as my legs could carry me without running like a moron, became my dad and his mom could see me. We quickly let go after a tight hug.

'Hello, Neel. Good to see you up again; we've been so worried about you,' Dad said, coming from behind me and patting Neel's shoulder.

'Hi, uncle,' Neel said, sounding rather guilty. 'I'm sorry for the trouble I caused at your house.' His eyes flashed at me for a very brief moment. 'I was not myself when I ran into your wall. It was stupid of me,' he finished.

No one said anything for a while; I guess they were all trying to take in Neel's inane explanation and it was definitely not making much sense to anyone. I felt so sorry for him and so guilty that I almost blurted out the truth. Except that the truth would have sounded even more bizarre.

'Hi, Neel. Good to see you in one piece,' Sonya interrupted just when my dad opened his mouth to say something. She sat on the bed next to me. Some of the tension in the air reduced.

Neel grinned at her. 'Yeah, thankfully. I've missed you too, doll.'

'Yeah right, you were in a coma. Like you could've missed anyone.' Sonya shrugged her shoulders.

'Why did you do that, Neel?' Dad asked abruptly.

I had known he would ask sooner or later. The I-was-stupid explanation was bound to be unsatisfactory. I bit my lip anxiously and looked at Neel.

Neel took a deep breath and closed his eyes. I wondered what he was trying to do. Pretend like he'd passed out? Nah. That was too lame.

His eyes fluttered open again. 'Uncle, I was in a panic when Li became unconscious and I was wondering what I could do to help her. I wasn't planning to bang my head into the wall. I was just walking around and—and thinking.' He faltered. 'It was an accident. I'll be careful next time,' he said and lifted his chin to look at my dad, full in the face, with so much confidence that suspecting him of lying would be next to impossible.

Dad frowned at him but nodded slightly. He was a man of few words so a nod was a common form of communication. I was relieved that Neel's explanation was officially accepted, though I was sure Dad still harboured a few doubts. Anyway, that would save him from further interrogation, I hoped.

I smiled at Neel encouragingly. I realised he didn't want

anyone to get involved and I was relieved that I hadn't told a single soul.

'Neel's getting discharged from here this evening. Would you like to come home for dinner tonight?' Neel's mom asked, a happy smile on her tired face. She looked from me to Sonya and then at Dad.

'So soon? After being unconscious for so long?'

She shrugged. 'The doctor says he is perfectly fine. He said there is nothing wrong with him—it was as if he was sleeping really deeply.'

I asked Dad, 'Is it okay if we go?'

'Sure. Let me know when you want to come home, I'll pick you up.'

'Umm, aunty, much as I'd love to come, I have a biology test tomorrow and I haven't really studied,' Sonya said tentatively. Dad shook his head and smiled fondly at his hard-working little daughter.

Neel's mom laughed. 'No, that's alright. You go home and study, darling. You can come by any other day.'

'Okay. Just save the tasty stuff for when I come,' Sonya joked and got up from the bed.

'You're going home?' Neel asked her.

'Yah. I'll see you soon, Neel,' she said and hopped over to hug him.

Dad walked over and gave him a farewell pat. 'Take care, son. We'll see you soon.'

Neel grinned like a thousand-watt bulb had been turned inside his head.

'Yes, uncle. Thank you for coming to see me today. Please tell aunty I'll come over to see her soon.'

'Thanks again for coming and bringing the kids. Good night.' Neel's mom walked Dad and Sonya to the door.

'Hey, what are you thinking?' Neel asked, his voice soft and slightly worried.

I looked back at him and smiled, thanking god for the hundredth time for the miracle that was before my eyes.

'I was thinking that it's good to see your mom alright again. You should've seen her that night.' I sighed, not wanting to bring that up right now. 'Actually, I hope you never see her like that. In other words, you're not gonna get hurt anymore.'

'I know. I feel awful for putting her through so much but I had to do that, Li. Otherwise, you could have been the one in a hospital and not me,' he said, shuddering a little.

'You really think he'd hurt me?' I asked. I wasn't sure if Omi had ever had the intention of hurting me.

'What are you talking about? He killed Jo!' he whispered frantically.

'Shh ...' I snapped, looking at the door where his mom and my dad were still talking. This wasn't the right time and place to talk about Omi. 'Listen, we'll talk about this when we're at your place, okay?' I whispered.

Neel's mom walked back in and closed the door behind her.

'The discharge is in half an hour. I'll just pack our stuff and then we're ready to leave,' she said cheerily and started clearing the bedside table.

There was a book too, which surprised me a bit.

'Didn't know Mum reads?' Neel teased.

'Actually, no,' I said and picked up the book. It was *Gone with the Wind*.

Neel's mom laughed. 'Where do you think Neel's love for literature comes from?'

'Neel's love for literature?' I snorted. 'Now that's a first.'

'Mum, that's your other son, not me!'

She chuckled and smacked his head with an empty bottle and ducked into the toilet with a cheerful 'Alright, I'll see you in few minutes!'

'Mum! Gross. Did you have to inform us?' Neel called out, scrunching up his nose disgustedly.

'Oh shut up! Like you don't shit your ass out,' I said.

'Two days without me and you people have become barbarians.' He threw up his hands in the air looking so much like his old self.

'What? Why you looking at me like that?' he snapped, one perfect eyebrow shooting up.

I realised I had been staring at him a tad too intensely. I mentally shook myself and looked at the book.

He cleared his throat. I could feel the awkwardness in the air rising again. Crap. This was not how it was supposed to be between Neel and me.

'How many times have you read that book?' he asked, slowly slipping back into bed.

He lay down and closed his eyes. Ohmygod. He looked so adorable.

'Just twice,' I said, purposely reducing the true number.

'So why you pretending to read it again?'

'Pretending? I'm not *pretending* to read anything. I love this book,' I snorted, trying to sound like I was pissed when in fact, I knew he could see through my excuse to not look up at him.

'Give it up, will you?' he chuckled. 'Talk to me.'

By the end of two seconds, I snapped the book shut and peeked at him. 'Sure. What do you want to talk about?'

'I don't know; not about him,' he said dismissively and opening one eye lazily, he asked, 'You have a crush on me, don't you?'

My jaw dropped. Well, that was unexpected. I quickly snapped it shut.

'Why—why would you think so?' I stuttered.

'Because you're acting all weird and the way you look at me …' he fished for words. He looked like he was enjoying this way too much. 'You seem to think that I'm hot.'

'You *are* hot. Like you have any doubts about that.' I shrugged, still trying to play cool.

'You know that's not what I meant.' He winked at me.

Gosh! This was *so* not Neel-like. I had never, and I mean *never*, seen him flirting with *any* female my entire life. And the fact that he was actually flirting with *me* was truly, *truly* hard to digest.

'You still remember what I told you before all this happened?' he asked me. His voice had lost the playful edge. Now he sounded vulnerable and … intense.

'That you just might be in love with me?' I couldn't help but smile back at him.

'Yes, that one.' He nodded and grinned.

'I know you *love* me. But … maybe you're just confused with everything happening now. I know you care a lot for me, Neel. Maybe you've just confused that with being in love with me?' I hoped I'd used the right words. Hurting his feelings was the last thing I wanted to do.

He beamed like he'd just won a million-rupee lottery.

'I knew that's what you'd be thinking. I know, as far as you or anyone else knows, I'm gay. And I really appreciate you trying so hard to put it in a way that would not hurt my feelings. And honestly, it doesn't hurt my feelings. But yes. I am in love with you.' He stopped and took a deep breath.

I blinked. Ohmygod. Neel Sarathy was in love with me. I knew that he wasn't lying. What was I going to say to him? That I was in love with him too?

But I wasn't sure. The only time I'd truly believed that I was in love was with Omi Daan. And he'd turned out to be an insane maniac who I was not even sure was real, who killed my best friend and was now trying to get to Neel.

'Won't you say something?' His voice was barely a whisper.

'Uh … I … Neel, I love you. I haven't figured out the "being in love with you" part.'

There. I told him the truth. That was all I could do.

'At least, you do find me hot in the *other* way?' I could hear the slightly disappointed note that had leaked into his playful voice.

I sat on the bed beside him. I stared at him, slightly narrowing my eyes and I sighed.

'Yes, you look very hot in the *other* way.'

He stared back at me. And then, he gulped very distinctly and reached for my hand. His hand was cool and soothing.

His other hand gently stroked my left cheek. For a moment, I remembered Omi. I quickly shook off this memory and looked back at Neel.

He was not smiling anymore. And then he scooted closer to me. He smelled good. And then before I knew it, he was kissing me.

It was nothing like I'd ever felt before. It was tender and *real*.

I didn't realise something was stirring behind me till Neel slowly pulled away, grinned and then hugged me.

I looked back and wanted to crawl under the bed when I saw Neel's mom staring at us like we'd dropped out of space. The folded newspaper tucked underneath her arm dropped on the floor. Slowly, her stunned expression turned to a half-amused, half-happy look.

Neel's grin only widened. He called out to her, 'Ma, I'm still me.'

She exhaled loudly and gave a shaky laugh. I could feel my face burning. I wanted to kick Neel.

'And I actually thought Neel was gay,' she said at last, shaking her head. She tried to hide the excited glint in her eyes but her grin gave her away. She walked to the chair and plonked herself down, her eyes moving from my embarrassed to Neel's very unembarrassed face. Another urge to kick him swept over me.

'I *am* gay,' Neel said matter-of-factly, amusement thick in his voice.

'He *is* gay,' I said immediately, bobbing my head up and down nervously. As if that was going to change anything that Neel's mom had just seen.

Neel snorted and put his arm around my waist. The nerve of him!

I couldn't read the expression on his mum's face but it seemed like she was … happy. Slowly, I pushed Neel's arm away from my waist and gave a nervous laugh, feeling like a complete moron. The awkward silence continued.

Then at last, Neel cleared his throat. 'Okay, so Li and I are slightly more than friends now. You don't have a problem with that, do you, Mum?'

'Of course not!' she exclaimed, too quickly. 'I knew it was going to happen … sooner or later,' she said, absentmindedly. She fished for her phone in her ginormous bag (as Neel liked to call it).

'Alright, kids. Akash just reached the hospital with my car; we can go home now. Get all the stuff together. I'll go finish up with the hospital formalities,' Neel's mom said and got up from the chair. 'And be good while I'm gone,' she added teasingly as she walked out of the room, her heels clicking rapidly on the tiled floor.

I gave Neel a dagger-like stare. He did his hair-flicking thing and hopped out of the bed, his lips still twisted in a cocky grin. When both his feet rested on the floor, he swayed a little. Worry washed over me as I helped to steady him.

'What are you thinking? You just can't jump out of bed in that condition! Are you ready to go home?'

'Gosh Li, will you chill?' he chuckled. 'Stop yelling at me like I tried to commit suicide. My doc's gonna come to check on me again before we leave.'

'Why did you try to get up then?'

'Because you looked like my mom had just announced

that the world was gonna end when she walked out. I wanted to hug you and tell you you don't have to be so embarrassed all the time!' he chuckled louder.

I sighed. This was going to take some time to get used to.

I suddenly remembered girls gossiping back in school about Neel being the most desirable gay guy ever.

'What? You're blushing!' He brushed my cheeks with his fingers.

'Oh, am I?' I tried to sound absentminded, like he was the last thing on my mind.

'Oh please, I know what you're thinking. You want to kiss me. Go ahead.'

I smacked his chest playfully and threw my arms around his neck.

Omi Daan

He flitted aimlessly through the arcade he had created between his own mind and that of Sonali. He knew he had to bring her back to him. He could feel her slowly slipping away from his grip. What was taking her so long to get back to her miserable longing for him?

The boy turning up was the last thing he had expected. He had underestimated the human; Neel's spirit was strong enough to enter the Realm without a Call. If only he had been a little weaker, Omi could have trapped him there and let him go only when his body had deteriorated beyond help. After that, his spirit would have fled and wandered helplessly from the terror of what his body had become.

And then, he sensed it. A flicker of heat and then something like a jolt. *No!* Omi flinched. He felt the new passion, the excitement, the … Omi tried to shut his mind from hers. He felt her *love* for him, for Neel.

And then something snapped. The connection was no more.

A thick wave crashed into him, bearing him down with its sheer weight. Omi fell to his knees. His thoughts crumbled all round him, his very being felt in tatters.

Omi tried to summon his scattered being back into one whole. Sonali could not, *would not*, break him down like this. Those were *her* emotions he had felt, they did not belong to him; they had no power to bear him down in any way.

Neel Sarathy. The Void whispered to him. The stench of Neel's spirit wafted over him. Omi cursed venomously. He realised his terrible mistake again; the boy was not to be underestimated. He had the potential to love like a normal human being was supposed to.

Now the game had to change.

Omi Daan.

A shrill cry cut through the stillness of the Void. Omi opened his eyes wider, alert. He knew who it was who called out to him. But he couldn't let himself be found. Not yet.

He had come too far to be held back from claiming Sonali. She was his. She would understand his need for her essence once she left her earthly form and joined him in this world.

The voice was persistent. Omi tried to shut his mind. He cursed in outrage as the Void did nothing but lie back as a silent spectator.

But *she* wouldn't give up; *she* who had reduced him to this. Anger seared through him as he shut his mind harder, raising higher walls and barricading his mind completely. Until, finally, he was alone again, safe in the cocoon of his mind which he had come to think of as invincible and unreachable, even to the sister who pleaded with him to set himself free, the sister of his long-forgotten childhood: Sonali.

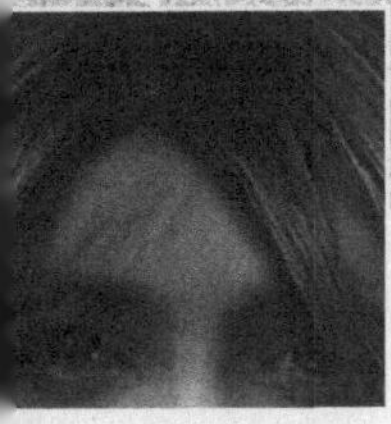

Sonali Machado

Three nights. And I hadn't dreamt of him, not once. I hoped my fears would not prove true. Somehow, I felt his silence foreboding—like the calm before a storm hit.

Neel never left my side. If he wasn't at my place, I was at his. Even Ma and Dad didn't bother to ask where I was going whenever I left the house. Off with her friend, they must have thought. It was pretty convenient that they were absolutely clueless about the latest development (heehee).

'Isn't that a good thing?' Neel asked.

'Yah, it is. But it doesn't feel … right.' My head felt heavy even when I spoke about *him*. 'I just feel like—like this is never gonna be over, Neel! I know that it's a good thing I don't see him in my dreams anymore but he's still out there. I can feel it. He's not going to stop.'

Neel pulled me into his arms and we sat for a long time, not saying anything. When words failed, only silence could comfort. I blamed myself for the millionth time, for the pain and trouble I was causing Neel, for Joanne Leslie.

I missed her achingly. Yesterday, we had gone to her grave and sat there for hours. And I had spoken to her in my heart.

'Jo, I am so sorry for this. I hope you have gone to a place better than any other you've ever known. I promise I'll still tell you everything that goes on in my life; you're still going to be with me when I laugh, when I cry, when I'm hurt, when I'm sad, when I'm ...'

'What do you think she would have said if she were here with us now?' Neel asked, an amused note in his voice. 'If Jo saw us together?'

'Oh.' I smiled dreamily. 'She would've said, "I knew this was gonna happen sooner or later", like your mum.'

'Did *you* think so?'

I looked up at him with my best flirty grin.

'Did you?' he asked me again.

'No, of course not. What about you?'

'I'm not sure but I think it was always in me and I realised it a few weeks, no *years*, too late.'

I looked down at the floor. He had been a few weeks too late. None of this would have happened if *we* had happened earlier. I wouldn't have spoken to Omi Daan if Neel and I had been together. Joanne would have been with us now, probably teasing our asses off.

'Hey,' he called.

I couldn't bear to look at him. 'It's not your fault,' I said softly. 'Not anyone's fault but mine.'

'Don't start with that again.'

'I have to go now. It's getting late,' I said abruptly and got up.

'It's alright,' he said immediately. 'Come on, I'll drop you home.'

'I can manage on my own.'

'I know you can manage on your own,' he snorted, 'but I'm not letting you go alone. Today's your lucky day; we're taking my mum's Scooty.' He gave me a lopsided grin and wagged his eyebrows.

'You're not serious!' I giggled. 'We're so gonna get busted. There are cops all over the place!'

'Come on, you really think I'd let them catch us? Now stop quacking and follow me,' he chuckled and took my hand, pulling me out of the room to the garage.

The night was chilly. I was shivering by the time we hit the road. I covered my head with the hood of my sweater and scooted closer to Neel.

'Oh my god, what's with the Eskimo look? It's such a nice night. Take off your hood, enjoy the breeze,' Neel shouted, trying to raise his voice over the sound of the traffic around us.

Suddenly, the Scooty skidded to a halt and we jerked forward. I hadn't seen the gigantic truck until it sped across right before us. Apparently, neither had Neel.

'Fuck!' Neel swore at the top of his voice, straightening his back. I was still too stunned to move. 'What, is he trying to kill us or something?!' Neel cried out.

A couple of two-wheelers around us stopped and checked on us. A few cars slowed down but didn't bother to stop, seeing that everything seemed fine.

'That was so weird. I didn't even see it coming!' I said, bewildered. My heart was still racing.

'I know, like he was sent from my personal hell to get me caught by the cops. I am *so* not gonna let that happen,' Neel bellowed and sped off with another jerk.

I clutched onto him tightly. The speed was exhilarating

but frightening at the same time. I imagined we were on a wild chase with the bad guys behind us. A giggle escaped and Neel joined in.

'I love you!' he hollered.

A few pedestrians turned to look at us. We burst into laughter.

'I love you too!' I hollered back at him.

'Check out that cop now.' Neel jerked his head to a burly cop standing at the junction of four roads. I prayed he'd be too occupied to notice two teenagers.

We passed by. And nothing happened. This inspired another round of cheering.

'Ballistic!' Neel exclaimed, exhaling in relief. 'One down, baby!' He winked over his shoulder and leaned further back.

I smacked a kiss on his cheek and ruffled his sleek hair.

We quickly reached the entrance to my lane. Neel skidded to a stop, brakes screeching against the asphalt.

The lane was pitch black. The main road and the adjacent streets had lights but all the lights on my lane were off.

The darkness felt alive. An iciness engulfed me and knocked my breath out. Neel cringed and grabbed my arms which were around his waist.

We said nothing for a long time.

The feeling creeping over me was strangely familiar. Something between reality and a dream, or worse, a nightmare. I felt my resistance slowly crumbling. I wished Neel would speak to me, make me strong. But even he seemed paralysed. My breath was coming out in gasps, a sense of surrender overwhelming me.

And then Neel snapped out of it.

He kicked the Scooty back to life, turned it around and shot back towards the main road.

I pressed my face to his back and clutched his waist. I couldn't remember what I was crying for, what we were fleeing from. I only registered the fear.

I knew who had been waiting for me.

Omi Daan.

Neel veered into another lane cutting from the main road and sped till we reached a dead end. He and I gingerly got off the Scooty.

He took two deep breaths. His eyes were on the ground and he didn't look up until his breathing was somewhat calmer.

'Are you okay?' I asked, reaching out a shaky hand to him.

He just stared at me and shook his head slowly.

He looked freaked. I wondered if he was finally losing his nerve. But there was something else in his expression. He was ... pissed.

'He can't do that.' His voice sounded hoarse and slightly breathless.

'Do you think it's really him?' I asked, knowing the answer, but still dreading to hear it from Neel.

Neel gently pulled me closer to him. 'I'm not sure. But I think I—I felt him. I felt like some kinda cold stuff was stabbing my chest and I was so scared it was happening to you too.' He pushed away the hair sticking to my face with the sweat.

'Why won't he let go?' I moaned. I was sick, so sick of being afraid, of being helplessly stuck with so much paranormal bullshit. 'I felt it too, you know. The cold stuff.'

Neel's body went rigid. 'You're not going home alone again,' was all he said, his voice thick.

How strong he had grown that he could actually knock the power off an entire street and make me *and* Neel feel the cold fear. But was it possible that he could take us down? *Together*? And would he really hurt Neel in the process of getting to me, as he did with Jo?

'Where do you think he draws strength from?' I asked Neel flatly, taking his hand in a firm grip.

'What are you talking about?'

'Omi Daan. How is it that he's stronger than before?'

Neel's eyes narrowed. 'I wish I knew that,' he said bitterly.

'You know what, Neel? I think the key lies there. If we can find out what makes him strong, maybe we can stop him! Think hard, Neel! Think about what he's said to you. There's got to be something he let slip.'

Neel ran his fingers through his hair. I knew I was doing a little too much badgering but I was too excited with what I'd just figured out.

He looked tired and apologetic. 'Come home for a sleepover. I can't think right now, I'm sorry. We'll talk it over dinner or something.'

'Sleepover? I've been at your place the whole day; my dad will be like *hell no!*'

'As if you didn't have a sleepover, like, almost every week at Jo's place?'

'You're a boy.'

'Gay boy.'

I snorted. He laughed. I nudged him to the Scooty.

'What if the power's not back?' He didn't give up.

I stopped. What if the power was still out? I remembered the terrible icy feeling that had almost numbed me in that dark. And then I thought of Neel. I couldn't risk getting him hurt anymore.

'I'll come to your place,' I said reluctantly.

We decided that we'd swiftly ride past my lane and have a peek to see if the lights were back. If they weren't, we were going back to Neel's place and I'd call up Ma and Dad with some excuse. Neel said it wouldn't be a problem talking his mom into talking to Dad for us.

My heart pounded faster and faster as we neared the lane.

'Hey, hang on,' Neel said, just loud enough that I could hear. I knew that he wasn't his bravest either.

Time seemed to slow down bizarrely as we reached the curve of my lane. The darkness loomed, pulsating and bloated with the light that it had swallowed up. A shiver ran up my spine and I averted my face, terrified of what I would see if I looked too closely. A glossy red car zoomed past me and I tried to distract myself, my eyes following it as it sped away.

I knew Neel was going to stop again. But this time, I knew I couldn't let that happen lest I lose him forever.

'No! Keep going, Neel. Eyes on the road!' I cried out, tugging him, anything to tear his fixed gaze on the darkness so near to us, almost touching us.

'Neel. Please!' I shrieked.

The Scooty rolled to a stop at the entrance of the lane where a beam of light slanted only a few inches away from us. Beyond that, the darkness revelled.

'Turn around. Let's go, please,' I whimpered, my throat

burning with every word that came out. It felt like hot coals had been shoved down my mouth.

Neel didn't say a word, didn't move. He just sat firm, not crossing the beam of light, his hands clenching and unclenching on the handlebars.

My pleas died in my throat. My vision started blurring. I couldn't remember when I actually saw no more.

But I could still hear.

And what I heard was *his* voice, calling out to me in the sweetest way that a voice ever could be.

I willed myself to shut it out. And then I felt nothing more.

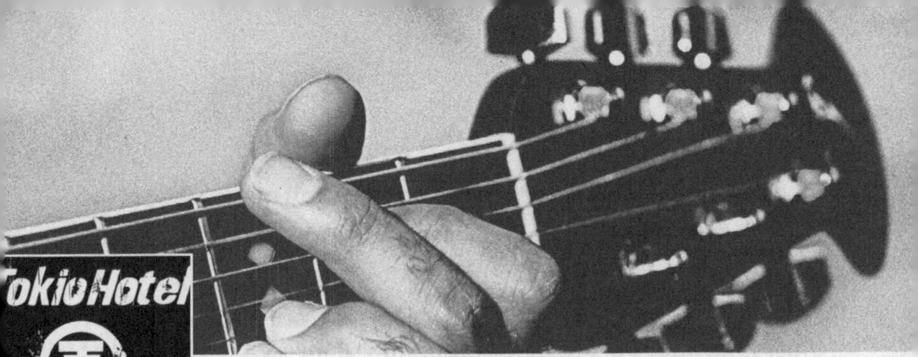

Neel Sarathy

My toes were the first thing I could feel, strangely numb and heavy. I twitched them in all directions. The tiny muscles stretched as much as they could and my body slowly regained consciousness.

A shock ran through the cloud of oblivion in my brain. I scrambled to my knees, only then realising that I had been knocked flat on the ground.

'Sonali!'

I couldn't see her.

The Scooty lay a few inches away from my feet, scraped and dented.

'Where the fuck are you, Li?' I called out again. Tears welled up, clouding my vision.

Light flickered above my head. My ears pricked to a distinct sound of an owl hooting. And then the whole lane was lit.

The sudden burst of light from all directions was piercing. I hastily shielded my eyes from the streetlights, which felt a million times brighter than they had ever been.

After what felt like a century of squirming under the penetrating light, I slowly took my hands off my eyes and peered around, still squinting.

A few feet from me, she stood so still I could have mistaken her for a wax mannequin, rigid and emotionless. Her skin was so white and translucent, I felt like I could almost see through her.

This was not good.

I took a deep breath and struggled to get myself up on my feet.

'Li? Are you alright, girl?'

Her eyebrows scrunched a little and her face only got whiter. I got a terrifying feeling that there was not an ounce of my Sonali in there. Eyes narrowed slightly, she puckered her lips disapprovingly.

I wondered why no people had gathered around us when it was obvious that we had met with an accident.

I hobbled towards her. A sick feeling filled me as she was still not moving or showing any sign of wanting to get to me.

'Hey, I was talking to you.'

I couldn't even catch the range of emotions that suddenly played on her face, like she was doing a ridiculous mime or something.

At first, she looked like she had been slapped, her nostrils flared like she was going to abuse me. And then, she looked completely spaced out, eyes glassy. And the next second, she began to cry as I have never seen anyone cry. Her lips pulled back and she bawled.

I stood rooted. This was *not* Sonali.

And then she fell on me, her body shaking so furiously I had to tighten my arms around her to hold her up.

'What the hell is going on, Li? Are you okay, girl?' I whimpered, feeling utterly broken seeing her like this.

She wouldn't meet my eyes.

'Talk to me. Please.'

She hung on to me. After a while, her sobs turned into wild hiccups. Her breathing slowed, becoming heavier. She shifted uncomfortably in my arms.

'The streets are empty, Neel,' she murmured abruptly against my ear. 'They're never empty.'

'I know.' I exhaled.

'The goddamn street is empty, Neel!' She pulled back and glared at me.

I couldn't help but give a little sigh of relief when I saw her eyes.

'Calm down, will you? I'm not blind. There's something abnormal going on alright.'

'But the good thing is, the lights came on,' she said, sniffing and throwing furtive looks at the streetlights.

'Yeah. Did the lights feel super bright when you woke up after the fall?'

She looked at me dubiously and frowned. 'What fall?'

Did she have a concussion or something? 'You see my Scooty over there? Remember we were riding that? But it's on the road now.' I pointed at the scooter lying pitifully, not far from us. 'We met with an accident, Li. I don't know how but I think I know who made it happen.'

'Oh,' she said at last, nodding slowly as if it was coming back to her bit by bit.

'Are you alright? Did you get hurt anywhere?' I asked her, taking her hand in mine.

'Hurt? No. I just remember standing here. And looking at you.'

'I know. And I hoped that you'd actually come and help me up or something.'

She blinked twice. 'I am so so sorry, Neel.'

She vaulted into my arms and almost crushed me.

'Are you hurt? Oh my god!' she cried. 'Are you hurt anywhere? Tell me.'

I hadn't noticed that I had been scraped like a chicken until she touched my bruises. I winced.

'Oh sorry! I'm only making this worse. Let's get home and take care of those bruises.'

'Yes, please,' I whimpered.

She put an arm around my waist and lifted my arm over her shoulder. We hobbled back to the Scooty.

She lifted the fallen Scooty briskly and started pushing it into the lane. I tried to keep up with her. She seemed to be filled with this sudden burst of energy

Strangely, there were still no people around.

'You think he caused this total desertion on your lane?' I asked.

'Yes, totally. But how'd you think he did that?'

'You're right, we really need to find out his source of power or whatever,' I snickered. 'Don't you think this is getting to sound more and more like the adventure shows for kids? Like the Power Rangers stuff. *Find out his source of power*. Seriously, it's kinda starting to sound funny to me when we put it that way.'

'Well, it's definitely not funny 'cause Jo died because of him and his source of power,' she said darkly.

'Hey, I didn't mean it like that. Okay, I'm sorry I said that.'

'No, I'm sorry, that was harsh. But you know what, it might sound childish but it's the truth. That's the way things work—with a source of power. And I'd do anything to find it and stop him before he hurts you or anyone else I love,' Li said, her hands slightly trembling, betraying the perfect control in her voice.

'You forgot someone.'

'Who's that?'

'You. You have to stop him from hurting you too.'

'Well, technically he never hurt me.'

'He put you in something like a mental asylum, Li.'

'Yeah. You're right. I just meant he hasn't hurt me physically.'

'It wouldn't have been too long before he did, if he still had such a hold on you.'

A few more steps and we reached her gate. The lights were on but it seemed like there was no one at home. Even the neighbouring houses seemed to be completely lifeless. A chilling unease spread through me again.

We stood still for a while, neither of us moving an inch.

'It's awfully quiet.' I didn't know why I whispered.

'Do you think we should wait until there's some movement inside?' she whispered back.

I sighed and nodded. Our eyes met and I could see the fear and worry in hers.

And then, with a sudden jolt, sound blasted from the house.

The television was so loud, I had to cover my ears. There was also distant radio music coming from the kitchen. A booming laughter filled the air, soon joined by a squeaky giggle. It was Li's dad and her sister.

I sighed in relief. She was beaming. I pulled her into a tight hug and we had the deepest kiss ever.

She giggled, pulled away and looked straight into my eyes. 'I think Omi froze time,' she said. She didn't seem horrified.

'He's *that* strong. We need to do something fast.'

I pulled her into an embrace again.

'Hey, hey. You do know we're right in front of my house, right?' she grinned at me impishly. 'And people are going to start appearing everywhere and start seeing everything and then eventually start talking everywhere like they always do.'

I chuckled and let her go.

It was strange to be so happy just like that, as if the ice blast and the fall from the scooter had happened ages ago.

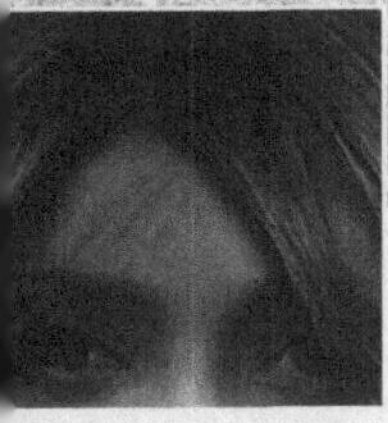

Sonali Machado

It's weird how you can miss a person so much when you know you're gonna spend just a single day without them. Maybe because we were also both constantly missing Joanne.

I talked to Neel for almost an hour as soon as I woke up. I had called just to check on him but the conversation had carried us away.

'Morning, sunshine,' my sister's voice drifted to me. She was standing near the door, holding a cup of something steaming and very inviting.

'That's for me?' I asked her.

'Sure, if you happened to be *me*.' She took a long noisy draught from the cup.

'You little ...' I murmured.

'I wanted to ask you something.' She pursed her lips broodingly.

'Sure. What about?' I stopped midway to the bathroom. 'Make it fast.'

'Okay, this might sound ridiculous. It definitely does to me but I have my reasons for asking. You know me, rationalist that I am ...'

'Cut the intro and ask already,' I snapped.

'You've been spending a lot of time with Neel lately.'

'Yeah, so? I always have.' I could guess the direction of this conversation. I wanted to see how long she took to actually ask me straight out.

'You guys are more than friends, aren't you?' she burst out.

I could still drag this on for a while. 'Why would you think so?'

'Because,' she said and paused, 'because there's something different in the way you look at each other now. And—and ... Something's definitely changed.'

'Have you seen us flirting or something?'

She gave me a confused look. I was thoroughly enjoying myself; it wasn't every day you got to toy with smarty-pants Sonya. 'Just tell me; yes or no.'

I chuckled, 'Yes, Sonya. Something's definitely changed. We're together.'

'I *knew* it! But wow, it's *so* weird.' She shook her head in disbelief. 'How'd it happen?'

I grinned at her. 'Let me go wash up and I'll launch into that.'

'Hello? Neel! Where the heck are you?' I screamed into the phone. This must have been the fiftieth time I had called him and he decided to pick up now.

'I'm so sorry. I should've told you before. I found something, Li. You've got to come home right now!'

'Okay, so you're at home now? Where the hell did you go? You should've sent me a text or something.'

'Hey, chill. I'll explain it to you—just come now.'

I sighed in relief. I was just glad he was home. 'Okay, I'll be there. Is it—is it about *him*?'

He didn't answer for a couple of seconds, but I already knew what he was going to say. 'Yes.'

I snapped my phone shut. I didn't know if this was supposed to be good news or not. What if finding more about him meant facing more of his mysterious shit which could have nearly killed us the previous day?

I brushed aside that thought. I couldn't waste time thinking about what he could do to us. I hurried to Ma who was fixing dinner and told her I needed to see Neel.

'What happened? Is he okay?' she asked, concern written on her tired face.

'Everything's fine,' I said tightly. My face would have made it obvious that it was otherwise.

She frowned, unconvinced. 'Okay. But don't be too late.'

Neel opened the door two seconds after I had rung the bell.

'Hi,' he breathed, crushing me into a hug. And damn, did it feel good.

'Hey.' I hugged him back warmly, happy that we still had small wonderful moments.

'I'm sorry, did I worry you too much?' he asked, still not breaking our embrace.

I sighed, 'No, not too much. Now tell me what's going on.'

He pressed his lips on mine briefly and then took my hand, leading me into the sitting room.

'Okay, now promise not to get mad at me?'

'Depends on what you did.' I narrowed my eyes at him. This was making me uneasy.

'Alright. I went to that bridge, where Jo had seen him. I remembered—umm—Jo telling me about that place and something made me wanna go check it out. The place isn't that far from here, just an hour on the bus. So it turns out that the one witness who saw this happen had lived near that bridge then, and she still lives there now. I spoke to her.'

'Witness? To what?'

I saw the excited glint in his eyes as he continued. 'Her name's Asha and she's a year younger than us. I was looking around when I got to the bridge, not sure of what to do. She'd been looking at me the whole time and then finally came up to me and asked what I was looking for. I don't know what made me feel like I could tell her what I was really there for, but I did tell her. That's when I got her to talk it all out.

'Omi killed himself, Li. He jumped off that bridge.'

I caught my breath. This was what we had suspected, but it was still unnerving to be told it was true.

'Omi wasn't alone when he committed suicide; there was someone else on that bridge, she said.' He eyed me meaningfully.

'His sister,' I whispered.

'Probably. But the strange part is, she saw the girl jump along with him but they never found another body down there, of course. And then the police decided that she must have been imagining the girl. But she told me that she was sure she saw the little girl.'

'Do you think Omi's parents believed that?' I asked.

'Well, maybe they did but they wouldn't have said that to the police. Their son committed suicide. They would have seemed deranged themselves if they spoke about their dead daughter's ghost.'

'Yeah. Point,' I muttered.

'I think his sister played some kind of a role in this. I think we should dig deeper in that direction.' He pursed his lips in thought.

'How do we dig deeper?'

'Maybe he's still trying to reach her; somehow, that's why he's still stuck in this state, whatever it is.'

'You think she drove him into madness? But she was only a sweet little girl who loved to draw small clouds with birds flying in and out of them,' I said dreamily.

I didn't realise how weird I must have sounded until Neel's silence grew awkward. 'What the fuck are you talking about?' he asked bluntly.

Nice. I guess he couldn't take any more weirdness.

'Nothing,' I said immediately, 'just something he used to tell me.'

'Okay. Please don't do that again.' He shuddered.

'Do what?' I asked, slightly offended.

'Be all warm and fuzzy when you talk about his family as if they're your own,' he said curtly.

'You know there's nothing wrong about his family; it's just him. They are victims, Neel. So is he, but he couldn't deal with it and he turned out like this.'

He scowled but said, 'Yeah I know, terrible things happened to them. I pity the parents. I mean, both their kids turned into these psychotic ghosts who now want to snuff the life out of other innocent people.'

I sighed. He was right.

'Why did he pick on you, Li? Just for your name?'

I looked at him. 'I don't know. I definitely had nothing to do with his sister's murder or his death.'

Neel slid his arm around my shoulder.

'No, he didn't have any reason to pick on me,' I said, a little more gently.

'Hmm ... your hair smells good,' he mumbled, pulling off the grip that held up my ponytail and burying his face in my wavy hair.

I giggled.

He pulled back and our eyes met. His caramel eyes sparkled like they had in the hospital when we first realised there was something between us.

The doorbell rang.

'Shucks, it's Mum.' Neel sat up, breaking the kiss. 'Perfect timing.'

I sat up, feeling a little lightheaded. A tiny giggle escaped me.

'Alright girl, behave now.' Neel winked at me and went to get the door.

'Hi Sonali!' Neel's mom breezed in, giving me a knowing smile.

Instead of blushing and cowering like I expected myself to, I beamed right back at her. 'Hi, aunty. How was your day?'

'Hectic. And this boy had to not answer his phone to add to the tension.' She narrowed her eyes at Neel.

'Look at me, Mum. I'm alright. I just went to check on some things. And I'm sorry. It won't happen again,' he said sombrely.

'Oh it's alright, baby. I guess I overreacted as well.' She sighed, placed her bags on the table and sat down on a chair heavily.

'Want something to drink?' Neel asked her and then winked at me.

I can't explain how much I liked it when he did that. When he winked at me while no one was looking, it kind of made me feel like we were truly part of this really special thing which involved no one else.

'Yes, please. Coffee will do,' she said and got back to rapidly texting on her phone.

'Come on, lend me a hand.' Neel half-dragged me to the kitchen.

I leaned against the wall and thought about what Neel had found out. Maybe no one had believed Omi when he talked about his sister's ghost haunting him. People must have thought it was emotional trauma or he was hallucinating or something. Did they try to get him help? Or maybe he never told anyone.

Pity surged through me.

'What are you thinking so hard about? Do you want some coffee too?'

'Yep, thanks,' I nodded. 'How does the sister come into the picture? It doesn't make sense to me.'

'Hey, easy there. We can't go hunting for another deranged ghost.'

'Huh. When we go hunting for him, we end up getting almost killed!' I snorted, frustration making me crabby.

Neel gave me my cup and went off to give his mother hers.

We had to find Omi Daan again. A weird knot formed in my stomach. It had been so long since I'd seen *him*. I could not afford to grow weak again in his presence, but what if I lost my mind again?

Oh! So many what-ifs! My brain felt like it was going to explode.

'Hey. How's the coffee?' Neel asked, slipping his arms around my waist.

I had to smile. Another brain was here to share all my anxieties and what-ifs. 'Yah, it's good. So what exactly is your master plan to reach him?'

'I'm not sure how we're gonna reach him 'cause he hasn't been nosing into our dreams lately. You think we should both try running into a wall?' He cocked his head to one side, grinning moronically.

I nudged him not too softly on his chest and rolled my eyes. 'Come on, be serious. That is not going to happen again! You almost died, you idiot.'

'But you may never have got out of that dream if I hadn't come. Face it, my moronic actions do have their uses.' He shrugged, still in a playful mood.

My gaze softened. He was right. I'd be lost without him. 'I know. You're my knight in shining armour.' I smiled at him. 'And I cannot do without you, so please let's call off the stunts.'

This made him laugh, but soon enough he grew serious.

'We need a game plan.' He chewed on his lip for a while and then continued, 'You think if we sat together and meditated to reach him, we'll get through?'

I frowned; that seemed unlikely. But it was worth a try, I guess.

'Alright, we could try that. It's so not fair, isn't it? So far, he's been the only one who could pull us into those dreams where we could see him and now, when we actually *want* to see him, we've got to try so hard.' I scowled.

'Actually, I don't think he's the *only* one who can pull us to a dream to see him. You see, when I did the wall banging and followed you, I don't think he had anything to do with that 'cause he was pretty darn surprised when he saw me. I got in through my own means. So it's possible to get to him without his help.'

He sounded so confident. I hoped he was absolutely right.

'So which part of it do you think made it possible? The pain or your—umm—will power?' I asked sceptically.

'You don't really think it's possible, do you?' he sighed. 'I think it was both.'

'So what do you propose we do, Neel? You were joking when you said let's hit a wall, weren't you?'

He snorted. 'Well, I was only half-joking.'

'Ah, splendid. Now we'll both end up with a concussion or something worse.' I grimaced.

'Like I said, Li. We've got to take chances if we wanna finish him,' he said hotly.

'Just out of curiosity, do you think it's really possible to end him? I mean, how many times can a person die?' I shook my head slowly.

'I only intend to send him to wherever he's supposed to be now,' Neel replied darkly, taking my hand and pressing it soothingly.

I nodded stiffly. This whole thing was seeming more and more pointless to me.

'Okay, first things first.' He clapped his hands and moved away from me. 'Let's finish up our coffee and then think of ways we can injure our skulls efficiently,' he said, almost too cheerfully.

A thought struck me. I wasn't proud of it, but I had to bring it up. 'Do you think ...' I paused, swallowing. 'Do you think narcotics could help?'

Neel's casual smile was wiped from his face. He seemed to consider it for a while and then shook his head rigidly. 'No. That's only gonna get us really high and screw us in the long run. We need strong heads for this, Li. And I mean it literally.' His smile was back and he winked. 'Whether we take on a wall or a deranged spirit.'

I sighed, relieved that he had brushed aside my thought.

He chuckled and slapped his hand lightly over my back, 'Come on, Li. No need to beat yourself up for that. It was just a thought.'

'Well, thoughts lead to actions eventually, right?'

'True. But don't worry, I'll strap you and send you to rehab when the time comes.'

'Oh, shut up.' I punched his arm. 'Like we don't have more important stuff to think about now.'

This seemed to amuse him even more. He brushed my hair aside and planted a soft kiss on my cheek.

'I love you, girl. Calm down, will you? We're gonna figure

this out together, okay?' he murmured, pressing another kiss on my forehead.

That was the best part about troubles pressing down on you. When you got the nice moments, they were magnified in their wonderfulness.

Omi Daan

Exhaustion.

Uncertainty.

Fear.

Insecurity.

Feelings that had become alien to him were now rushing through his head, threatening to smother him under their intensity.

Too much of his strength had been drained. And it had not caused the damage he had imagined. Sonali and her little pet Neel were only growing stronger and their attempts to ward him off were getting more effective.

Patience. The Void chided him. Omi could feel the disapproval underneath.

No, he couldn't appear weak before the Void. He drew himself up. He wouldn't succumb to the uncertainty. He needed to think his way through and find a way to get rid of the boy. He was like a cockroach. Omi hadn't forgotten those disgusting little creatures that were so hard to kill.

He hadn't forgotten anything about the world he used to live in: the feel of the rain soaking his skin, the smell of dust in the wind on his face. The cool night that hosted millions of stars in their huge clusters. Oh, he even remembered the names of those constellations that mesmerised him—Orion's Belt was his favourite and he never missed the Little Dipper.

Licking chocolate and ice cream as they dripped down his fingers. Basking in the warm, glorious sun. The feel of sand between his toes as he sprinted on the beach.

I could send you back to that wretched place you came from, the Void told him, harsh and indifferent.

Omi froze. Slowly, it sank into him. Go back to that world? Was it even possible?

There must surely be a catch somewhere. The Void was not charitable. He listened, careful not to spill any of his thoughts to the Void.

What was the meaning of going back to the world of the living? Would he be alive? Did it matter anymore? He could only claim Sonali in this state. It was only here that he knew he could contain her.

But if he returned, he could feel and taste and *live* again. Maybe Sonali would forgive him for what he had done to her insignificant friend; maybe they could be together. Nothing truly mattered more than *living*. This time, he wouldn't be so hasty to give that up.

I want another essence.

Omi grimaced. The catch.

He could never really understand the Void, couldn't decide if it was a person or a place or a force. He only knew that somehow the Void gave him power and opened portals to the dream worlds where he had taken Sonali. When he had killed that weakling Joanne, the Void had been there, throbbing in anticipation. The Void had claimed her essence but it had also given him more—killing her had raised him to a higher dimension of power than he had ever thought possible. He could only imagine what killing another person could take him to.

Whose essence would satisfy the Void's insatiable thirst for power and vitality?

The boy, that lowly Neel Sarathy. Finishing off Neel would leave Sonali vulnerable. Finally, she would belong to him and him alone.

No.

Whose essence then? As a boy, Omi had loved surfing on the internet like every teenager. Making new friends on Facebook. The Void had made him realise its enormous power—and the world's audacity. To expose their individual essences, openly inviting beings such as him, to choose the one they wished for.

Among those billions, Sonali's essence had stood out, the only one that appealed to him. He was obsessed with her essence, addicted to it. The fact that she shared his sister's name and came from his city suggested that it was meant to be, she was destined for him.

I want her essence. Your sister's.

Omi Daan froze again. Her essence in exchange for his life?

However much he wanted to hide from her, did he want her to be trapped in the Void? She was still only a baby, a baby he'd sworn to protect.

She's lived longer in your state than you have. She's strong. I want her.

'Why not the boy? He's strong too. You've felt his essence,' Omi hissed.

Omi felt something unidentifiable emanating from the Void. It took him a moment to recognise it. Laughter?

The boy's essence is nothing *compared to your sister's.*

Dark thoughts broiled within him.

Reach out to her now, follow her voice. Bring her into me and trap her here. Then I shall open a doorway for you to the living world.

A second chance at life was worth any price.

And then, like peeling off his skin, he slowly let down the barriers that he had created in his mind. Focusing on one essence alone, he waited for her voice to call him again, the voice that was never far from the precipice of the Void.

He didn't have to wait long.

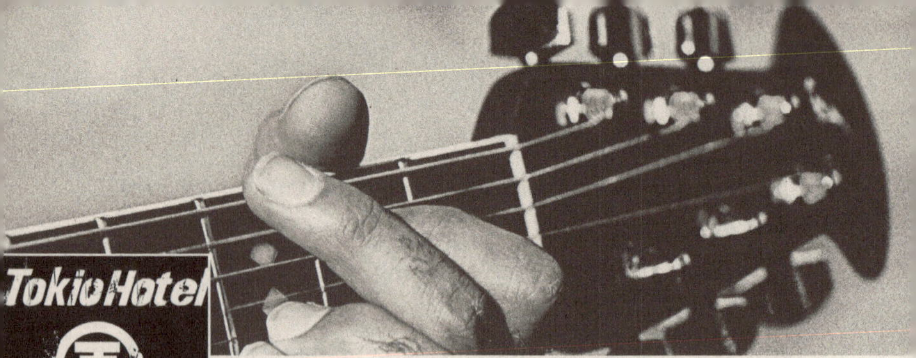

Neel Sarathy

After I made sure Li had reached home safe, I spent some quality time in the bathroom. My bruises slowed me down a little but by the time I was finished with my hot shower, I felt a whole lot better.

After dinner and doing the dishes, I strolled out on the balcony. I plugged my earphones and listened to some Evanescence. Summer nights were the best. A cool breeze brushed against me.

On the road below, I saw a couple of guys in a major face-off. I'd heard rumours of gang activities in our area but never actually seen any action. I eagerly unplugged my earphones.

I should admit. It was pretty cool.

These guys weren't actually rearranging each other's faces but were mouthing each other off really loud. I picked up a few things that they said. Girl trouble.

I glanced over to the other side of the road, looking for nothing in particular and ended up spotting someone who was definitely looking up at me in particular.

I did a double take and clutched the railing.

It was him.

Omi Daan.

Standing right below a streetlight, his face was illuminated in a way that made him look even more beautiful and bizarre.

We stood looking at each other for a really long time, like we were having a glare-off or something. I rubbed my eyes twice, making sure I wasn't hallucinating. And he didn't back down either.

A strong gust of wind blew dust right into my face and I had to throw an arm in front of my eyes.

And when I looked up again, he was gone.

I looked around frantically but there was no sign of him.

I cursed loudly. The gangster dudes gave me odd looks and moved a few houses away.

I had a feeling the shit had just crossed some serious lines I never expected it to. I'd just seen Omi Daan in the real world. At least, it had felt pretty real to me, unlike the mirror sighting I had in the train long back.

Not good at all.

I darted back into my room and grabbed my cell phone.

'Li. We're so fucked.'

'Figured that a long time back but what exactly are you referring to?' she answered coolly.

What was she so nonchalant about? Omi Daan was gonna get our asses kicked and it was going to be sooner than we'd expected.

'I saw him right outside my house. I swear it was him. And then he just went off. Disappeared. And I'm telling you it was *real,*' I told her in one breath.

She didn't say anything for a heartbeat.

'That's not possible. How can you be so sure that it wasn't another of his mind tricks? He's really gotten into your head. You can't let that happen, Neel.' She was whimpering by the end.

Okay, she wasn't taking this well. 'Hey, calm down, alright? No, it wasn't any of his …' I searched for the words she'd used, 'mind tricks, okay? I can tell the difference by now. I don't know how he came back to life, but he's back. As freaky and impossible as that is, we need to be more careful. But on the upside, he's not some unreachable spirit anymore, Li. That's got to count, right?'

She made some impatient noises. 'Yah, that's an advantage, I guess. Makes him more accessible to us if only we know where he is and how to catch hold of him.'

She must have been feeling so much more insecure at that moment. That creep could be strolling around to her place even as we spoke. Now I could feel the chills running up my spine.

'I have a feeling he's going to be the one coming to *us*. He's probably here for a reason. Okay, don't freak out but I'll tell you what I think.' I paused to make sure she was not having a bout of hysterics. 'I think he's here to kill me. He obviously didn't get too far with his plan of eliminating me as a spirit, so he's taking matters to a different level now.' I sighed, kinda surprised that I wasn't scared or anxious or anything.

'Neel,' she moaned on the other end, 'how can you be so cool about this whole thing?' Her voice dropped to a whisper. 'Do you really think he's completely human now?'

'That's what we're going to find out. But how on earth

did he turn human?' I muttered, feeling helpless with every passing moment. I couldn't let this overwhelm me. Not now.

'Do you think he struck a bargain with someone who is in change of souls? Like in *Ghost Rider*?' she asked dreamily. 'Do you think there's some kind of director who manages which souls can return to the world and which ones pass on to hell or heaven or some in-between place? But I guess he rarely permits them to come back. I mean, how often do we see dead people digging themselves out of their graves, and next thing we know, they're hanging out with us, chilling and watching TV and all.' She gave a not-so-sane giggle.

I don't know what scared me more at that moment: Omi back from the dead or this creepy version of Li. 'Li!' I yelled. 'Will you stop that! *Please* pull yourself together.'

She shut up completely. There was a moment's silence. Then she spoke calmly. 'Sorry, I kind of lost it there. It happens. Sorry if I freaked you.'

'Well, let's not lose it too much now, shall we?' I swallowed. 'I'll call you back, okay?'

I needed to think. Hell, I didn't have any kinda brilliant plan to work through, but I suddenly felt the need to get my mind working. Alone. Maybe it was too much for Li to take. We needed some time off for now.

'Okay. Call me if you need to talk.' She sounded really offended now.

Damn. What did I do?

'Yeah, sure thing. I love you. Good night,' I told her softly.

There was a click as she hung up the phone.

Omi Daan

He'd seen the boy, exactly like his dream self.

Omi reminded himself that he was a boy too. Well, not as young as he was when life had slipped from him. But his body was still young, though his mind had grown older. A pity he couldn't return in the form of a slightly older person. But what better way to win back Sonali's heart than the form with which she'd fallen in love?

What in the hell was he going to do in the middle of this city, which felt strange with all its activity and bustle?

His senses felt heightened—all the colours, scents and sounds were brighter and bigger. It was as if he wanted to take in as much as possible of the world as he could, every single second. It was almost too much.

Omi shook off the feeling of helplessness that was creeping into him. He needed a place to sleep tonight. And it was only now that he understood that feeling tugging in his abdomen, making it rumble every now and then.

He realised in astonishment that hunger would now be one major concern of his life as a human being every day. He had no money, he mused, but he needed to get some food.

He stopped in front of a building with a huge billboard and a clown sitting on a bench outside. The smell—the smell was instantly familiar. Yes, he remembered, going with his family for his birthday, or was it his sister's?

A group of young girls scuttled out of the door noisily. Before he could comprehend what he was doing, Omi found himself eyeing them as they paused to chatter and giggle. It was almost like with the smell of food—he just felt *drawn* to them. Especially the girl in a lilac top with a low neckline and tight jeans …

He saw that she too was studying him intently. Her lips were curled into something he couldn't quite make out: a smile or a mocking smirk.

She whispered to the girl next to her. The friend immediately snapped her gaze towards him, and smiled. This one, he felt, was mocking.

Omi felt his stomach protest again. He walked to the door and went in. In his peripheral vision, he could see the entire group gawking at him through the glass.

He stood still for a while, taking in the ambience of the place. There were many tables, most of them full. Somehow, Omi knew that he had to go to the counter and take food on the red trays.

It was all coming back to him.

Omi briskly walked up to the shortest queue and waited cheerily, smiling at anyone who happened to look at him for more than two seconds. And then it was his turn at the counter. A pretty girl with a high ponytail looked up at him and smiled.

'Yes, sir? What would you like to order?' she asked in a squeaky voice, her smile not wavering.

Omi hesitated, looking at the menu listed on the wall.

'Sir?' she asked again when he didn't respond immediately.

He could not really make out what the names meant, but again, memory came back.

'I'll have the chicken burger meal, thank you.' Omi flashed a brilliant smile, which stunned her for a fraction of a second. Then she got back to work, typing something into the machine in front of her and trying her best not to look his way.

'Anything else you'd like?' she asked cheerily, still keeping her eyes down.

'Please look at me,' Omi said politely, with just the hint of a smile but his eyes teasing.

The girl snapped her head up at him, her eyes widening like she couldn't believe what he had just told her. Her face puckered slightly in puzzlement.

Omi leaned further in, not taking his eyes off hers, and speaking very softly. 'I'm sorry to cause any inconvenience to you, but I don't have any cash on me right now.'

It was as if the girl was seeing the sun for the first time. A worshipful smile lit up her face and she nodded and hastily fixed his order.

Omi marvelled at himself. How had he known what to do? How had it worked? Some of the power of the Void lingered in him. He was not merely human, he was superhuman.

The girl handed him a tray with a burger packed neatly, some fries, a cup of Pepsi and few packets of ketchup.

She smiled and stood rooted in her place until he broke

eye contact with her. Omi moved away from the counter to a table at a far corner. When he looked back at her, she was holding her head with one hand and the counter with the other. A customer was yelling to get her attention but she seemed oblivious.

He could *really* get used to this, Omi thought smugly. Life had just begun again. And this time, nothing was going to stop him from getting what he wanted.

Sonali Machado

I felt guilty after I hung up on Neel. Maybe it was the nerves or maybe it was because he'd sounded like he was a little scared of me. Like I was some freak.

A chill ran through me. Was I losing my sanity?

I paced about my room, wondering if I should just call Neel and apologise for hanging up.

I stomped back to my bed and sat down heavily. No, I wasn't going to call him up. He said he needed some time to think, right? So it would be best if I just left him to that.

I turned off the lights and snuggled into bed, waiting for sleep to take me away from the mess of my waking life. The comforting part was I knew that Omi couldn't peep into my dreams anymore. He was as real as me now.

My PC made a sort of noise, like an engine kick-starting. The monitor sprang to life. I gave out a shrill cry as I watched in horror.

When my Facebook homepage opened, I willed my eyes to shut. I knew where it was going next. I knew whose face was going to stare at me from the screen.

What a fool I had been to think that it was all over! How

soon I had forgotten the terror of what Omi Daan could do. I squeezed my eyes tighter, afraid that they would open to more terrifying things.

I heard the pop of a chat box being opened. My heart thudded faster. Another pop and I clamped my mouth shut with both my hands to stop myself from shrieking out.

What could he possibly want from me now?

Only one way to find out.

I steeled myself. I balled my fists to stop shuddering. Don't be a coward, I said to myself. And then I opened my eyes.

Li

Come and meet me.

I didn't have to ask where because my eyes fell on his cover picture. It was a garden this time, lush with flowers of all kinds and a fountain brimming on one side. I knew exactly where it was: the flower show in Lalbagh.

I sucked my breath as realisation hit me. I took a deep breath and swallowed. I walked up to my desk, sat down and typed the first thing that came to my mind.

Me: Is it true? Are you really alive now?

Omi: Li, you know I've always been alive.

I could sense the playfulness. He still thought he could toy with me. I narrowed my eyes and pressed on.

You know what I mean. Are you absolutely alive?

He didn't reply for a couple of minutes. I waited stiffly, unable to exhale in anticipation.

Omi: Yes.

Me: So where are you?

Again a pause. This time it was longer. Of course, he wasn't going to give himself away so easily.

Omi: You know I've missed you, right? ☹☹

Anger surged through me.

Me: Then why did you try to kill me?

Omi: Is that really what you think?! ☹ You've become less smart than I remember. Maybe it's because of that worm you've been hanging out with.

Me: Guess what? He's my boyfriend now. You're going to leave him alone, okay? And you're going to leave me alone too.

Omi: Yes, I heard. So when did the happy realisation dawn, huh?

I could feel his cold spitefulness. I tried to push away the fear that had started to creep into me.

Me: Thanks to you, actually. We found what we always had for each other.

Omi: What you always had for each other?! Hahahha!

Like that was the biggest joke he'd ever heard.

Omi: Now that's bullshit. You just think you're in love with each other because times were hard and you stuck together. You've always loved him like a friend and brother; you know that. He's gay, for goodness sake, Li!

I shook my head in denial.

Omi: It's just a phase you're going through. It'll be over before you know it.

I frowned. What Neel and I had was real. I didn't need to listen to Omi telling me what to feel.

But then again, what if this was a phase Neel was going through? I pondered uneasily. Feelings of uncertainty clogged my mind.

Omi: See? You can't rely on something like that, love.

Again, that uncanny knack of reading my mind. My breathing grew rapid as I remembered the earlier times. No. I couldn't let him get into my head again.

Me: How do you know? You are human now.

Omi: I'm not very different from what I was, Li. I just have a human body now, which is quite a task to maintain, by the way.

Me: What about my friend who you killed? Do you know what pain you caused me?

There was a long pause. Then the words flowed fast.

Omi: Don't talk to me about pain. Do you know the pain I have been through to come to you? The unimaginable power I have given up? The one person who loved me whom I sacrificed? The anguish of feeling your soul shredded to pieces and then slowly stitched back one piece at a time, each moment stretching to centuries?

He'd gone through living hell to be with me. There was suddenly great joy in my heart.

But then, what about Neel?

Neel was a part of any plan *I* was ever going to be in. We were together now.

No more happily-ever-after thoughts about Omi and his pain. It had all been a mistake in the first place and not just a mistake, it went against the laws of nature. I mean, being involved with a ghost who's back from the dead? *Not* right.

With a new determination, I replied.

Me: You know what you're doing is not right. Can't you just let go of whatever grudge you have against life or whatever it is? You had your chance, Omi. And I'm sorry you blew it but you can't keep punishing me and the ones I love for what went wrong with your life. We have ours to live and you've already taken away one. Please stop it. This does not make any sense.'

Omi: Don't you think a person can have a second chance when he's messed up, love?

I was silent, rage boiling.

Omi: I love you, Sonali. There it is, simple and real. And that's the whole deal. I'm just a boy who fell in love with you. I don't know why you just see me as sinister, bloodthirsty and looking for a kill. I've told you so many times that I wouldn't hurt anybody as long as I know you're mine.

Me: It's not gonna work on me anymore, Omi. Don't even try!

Omi: I'm not trying anything, love. I know you still feel for me deep down inside. Stop holding back ... Everything's going to be perfect. We're going to be together, baby. You remember our dreams? Our dreams of being together ...

Me: Noooo!

Omi: Do you not remember? I know you do. And I remember every single moment of them. You know how real they were, you know we really were right together. Don't you want to live them in person now? Don't say no.

Me: STOP IT!

Omi: I know you, Li. I can make you happy forever. We can spend every moment together. Just like in the dreams. Isn't that what you yearned for? Isn't that what you used to moan and cry and wish for? It's going to happen now, baby! ☺

A warm sensation shot through me as I recalled how we spent every moment together in those few days when everything I knew was only him. Now we could live them for real. I could even touch him for real …

Maybe that's why he came back!

To be with me.

Maybe he wanted another chance at living, to spend it with me.

His face flashed before my eyes: that brown tousled hair, mesmerising grey eyes that seemed to be as old and faraway as the stars, the skin that felt like dewdrops.

Me: Are you that beautiful even in real life?

Omi: Hehehe. That's for you to let me know. When can I see you?

A maddening desire to see him took over, possessing me. How had I ever wasted a single moment thinking that it was possible not to see him when he was this close now? I'd been a fool to think that I didn't need Omi Daan anymore.

I swallowed—everything was a haze now. This feeling was strangely familiar. I could feel my mind slipping—soaring.

Me: Now!

Omi: Heehee baby! It's eleven in the night!

Me: I don't care.

I was definitely out of my mind now.

Omi: No, I'll see you tomorrow. ☺

Me: Promise?

Omi: Of course. Why do you think I came back, love?

I couldn't decide if that was a rhetorical question.

Omi: I came back for you.

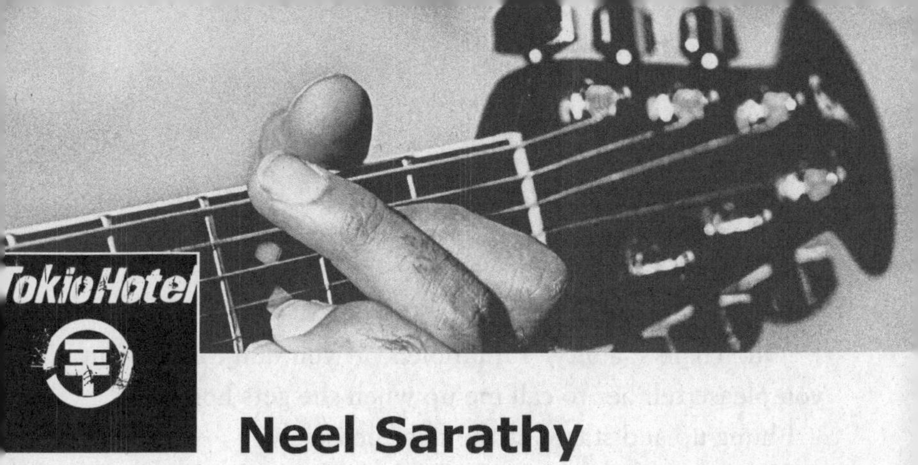

Neel Sarathy

I was one call away from grabbing the scooter key and going over to Li's place.

I had called eleven times, but she still hadn't picked up the phone. I texted her but, of course, she didn't reply.

Finally, I tried her landline, which I should have done five phone calls back. I just didn't want to come across as paranoid to her family and I had been behaving oddly enough.

'Hello?' It was Li's mother.

'Hi, aunty. This is Neel. I'm sorry to bother you but I've been trying to reach Li and she hasn't been answering. Can I please speak to her?'

I bit my lip. I hope I hadn't got her mum worried but I needed to know she was alright. And by 'alright', I meant not within a five-mile radius of Omi Daan.

'Oh, she's gone to meet some schoolmates ... Cherrie. She mentioned some others too, can't remember. She left in the morning and said she'd be home by five in the evening.'

Huh.

That was weird. I was usually the one to set up a get-together like that and *I* wasn't invited? Cherrie and the others would never do that.

I smelt something really fishy.

'Oh. Thanks, aunty,' I mumbled. 'If you don't mind, can you please tell her to call me up when she gets home?'

I hung up and stared at the floor pensively.

She was with Omi Daan.

I felt like I'd been stabbed on my spinal cord.

After everything that had happened, I couldn't believe this was her choice. Omi had become human. That didn't change anything. He was still a cold-blooded murderer.

What if he'd forced her into seeing him?

I started pacing around my room, my thoughts spinning.

A light knock on my bedroom door distracted me.

I stared at the door in disbelief. I was the only one in the house.

I gulped.

I kicked myself mentally and trudged up to the door.

No one. I must have been imagining it.

I sighed, relieved, shut the door and resumed pacing.

Thud! Thud! Thud!

It sounded like someone was trying to ram down my door.

My heart was pounding. I sprinted to the door and opened it wide.

A wave of stale air hit my face. Our house never smelt like that.

No person. No animal. Nothing.

'What the heck,' I muttered, dazed and feeling like I was somehow missing something here.

I turned, and she was standing right there.

It was a little girl, her hair braided into two plaits and wearing a slightly tattered maroon dress. She scrutinised me questioningly with big eyes.

Maybe she'd knocked the wrong door, I hoped. I knew it was not that simple. We had meshes on every window and I myself had locked both the doors of the house.

'Care to tell me how you broke into my house?'

'I didn't break into your house. I just came to see you,' she answered coolly.

'Yeah? How did you get in?'

'Out of thin air.'

She smiled at me serenely and walked to my bed. She folded her arms and sat down like an obedient kid.

Out of thin air?

Bizarrely, it made sense. I would have heard if she had tried to break in through the doors or the windows. The only thing I'd heard was that knock and the ramming sound against the door.

Damn. I *so* didn't need more craziness.

'Okay. Who are you?' I moved closer and stood in front of her, tall and slightly intimidating, I hoped.

She didn't flinch one bit as she looked up at me. 'I can help you,' she said calmly.

'With what?'

'With my brother.'

She turned away from me and started studying my room.

My jaws dropped and I moved a step back and gasped. 'You're Sonali? Omi's sister Sonali?'

She nodded.

'Wow. Unbelievable.' I shook my head.

She stopped looking around my room and turned to look at me, an adult seriousness on her face.

'He trapped me but I escaped. He shouldn't be here. And he should never have ended up in the Void either.' There was deep sympathy in her voice.

'The void? What's that?'

'The Void is a very powerful force. I've managed to stay away from its magnetic pull. But Omi fell prey to it. The Void drains our essence, twists our deepest desires, makes them urgent and burning and also gives unimaginable power.'

'Well, I don't see why anybody would say no to that,' I mumbled.

'Everything the Void gives, it takes back tripled. No essence can rest in peace if it is part of the Void. You'd do well to remember that, when your essence is freed from its earthly form.'

I shuddered. What was this? After-life lessons?

'Have you heard from your friend?' There was concern in her voice.

'Li? No, I haven't and I'm worried sick.' I paused. 'She's with *him* now, isn't she?'

'Yes.'

'Do you know where they are now?'

'Yes.'

'Are you going to tell me?'

'Yes. But you need to be prepared. You have to remember that he's powerful.'

I felt like charging out of the room right then. But she was right, I needed to know what to do.

'Right. So, you got any suggestions?'

'Yes. Why do you think I'm here?' she rolled her eyes.

Sarcasm. Nice. 'Fine, princess. Shoot.'

It was not much of a plan. She was going to tell me where Omi and Li were and I was going to attack him. She warned me that he was very powerful and he could easily make me walk away as soon as I turned up there.

Sonali doubted that he would be using any compulsion on Li, which made me feel betrayed. But then, that was just what she thought, and she could be wrong. Somehow, I knew she was right, though.

Sonali would step in and try to convince him that he didn't belong in this realm anymore. Gosh, I felt like I was going to get into some celestial war.

'Have you never spoken to him after he died?' I asked, feeling sort of uncomfortable to talk about such things. Those were things I used to laugh at.

'No. I spoke to him before he died,' she told me sadly.

'So you really were there with him. Was it really because of you that he killed himself?'

Something flashed in her eyes that made me want to hide under my bed.

'My brother was grieved,' she said tightly. 'And all my parents did was smother him by telling him that it was wrong to grieve. They tried to push aside my memory because of the pain it caused them. He collapsed mentally and he never got alright. My parents didn't see that he needed help, and even if they did, they did not want to acknowledge it.' She laughed bitterly. 'I couldn't get through to him, until—until that moment when he stood on a bridge, looking down at the water and thinking it was the only way he could free himself from the torment he was going through.'

I patted her lightly on the back. I was surprised that I could actually touch her.

'I begged him not to do it. I cried out to him, I even tried to pull him away. He thought he was imagining me, and he smiled at me, telling me that he was going to join me soon. And then he jumped.'

'What if you can't convince him to stop?'

'You kill him.'

I fell out of my chair in surprise.

'You're not serious.' I gawked. I knew I couldn't afford to have a panic attack now but she really wasn't helping in any goddamn way.

She shrugged and pursed her lips. 'Sit down.' It sounded like an order.

I got up and sat on the chair.

'Omi Daan is as dead as I am. He cannot live like one of you, try as he might. He's a toy in the power of the Void. He needs to be stopped before he destroys and manipulates more people. And the only way to do that is to kill him.'

I understood her reasoning but I couldn't imagine myself killing someone.

'It's the right thing to do,' she told me softly.

I felt stupid because it had never occurred to me that I would have actually needed to kill him.

'How?' I croaked, not taking my eyes off my hands.

'I suppose you won't be able to get your hands on a gun.

So, a kitchen knife would do,' she said, sounding too close to cheerful.

I couldn't help but give her a disgusted look. She got up and stood in front of me, her face a few inches away from mine.

'Even if I convince Omi to go back to where he came from, the Void will take him back and he may come back again. Kill him now, you sever his link to the Void forever. His essence will go where it belongs. He will never be able to reach you again.'

I nodded. I knew she was right, but the thought of it still filled me with dread.

'I love my brother. I want his essence to rest. Only then can mine.'

'Just out of curiosity, why didn't his essence go to where it belonged in the first place?' I asked her.

She threw me a tired look as though she'd been answering the same question for centuries.

'I'm sure you've heard of the wandering souls—the kind that know no rest until they acquire a sense of completion. My brother is one of those. His thirst for life and anything to do with the living drives him on. So you see how he ended up with the Void.'

She walked towards the window and gazed outside. A slight drizzle was falling now.

'Say I go to kill him. Won't he read my mind and try to stop me with his mind control?'

She smiled. 'That's where I'll help you. The Void is not the only force with power.'

'Oh please, don't tell me you're affiliated to another

mystical, unknown source of power,' I said, rolling my eyes but feeling very uneasy.

'Power by itself is pure and full of potential. It can only be tainted by the essence that wields it.'

'Okay.' I really didn't understand but whatever. 'So when do we get started?'

'Excellent weather. Excellent plan. I say, right now.'

I couldn't decide if that was another shot at sarcasm or she really meant that the drizzle was excellent and killing Omi Daan was the best plan she'd ever come up with, though the latter was probably true.

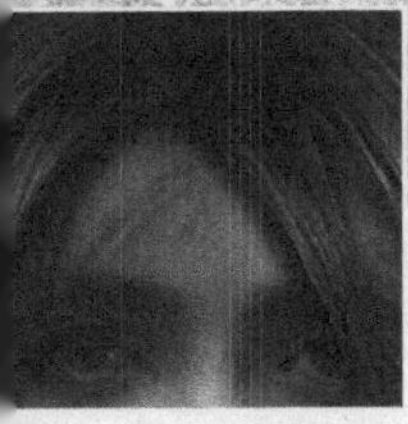

Sonali Machado

He was wearing a brown leather jacket, black jeans and an ivory t-shirt. A watch peeped out from under the cuff of the jacket—a Rolex, I noticed in my nervousness.

I had never seen someone so beautiful.

'Omi—Omi Daan?' I asked, though I had never been more sure, and smiled tentatively.

He nodded and smiled, looking slightly distracted. He reached out a hand fluidly and I took it slowly.

He kissed it softly, his eyes fixed on mine. And still holding my hand, he said, 'Finally. Nice meeting you, Sonali. You just made my day.'

'It's nice to meet you too,' I breathed, almost inaudibly.

He belonged here. As much as I belonged to him.

He leaned over and his lips touched mine.

I'd never imagined I could feel so much bliss.

I closed my eyes, listening to the water gushing from the fountain nearby where we sat together cross-legged, leaning back-to-back against each other. The grass we sat on was smooth and cushiony; I ran my fingers through it, letting the blades linger between my fingers. Meanwhile, Omi played with the strands of my hair that fell on his shoulders, humming a very old tune I couldn't quite follow but recognised vaguely.

Everything was utterly pointless and futile compared to being with him—alone, like this.

I looked up the sky as a flock of birds flew overhead in a V formation. I often wondered if they kept yelling at each other to 'hold the line' like in a drill; they always kept it flawless though. The sky was turning red now, making the clouds look like massive blood-soaked cotton balls.

'What are you thinking, Li?' he asked caressingly, his voice seemed to be one with the breeze.

'Just how happy I am, right here with you.' And it was true.

He shifted abruptly, making me fall smack onto his lap. I didn't bother to get up immediately; instead, I gazed into his enticing grey eyes.

'What? What are you thinking now?' I asked him.

'Just thinking of how this day is already coming to an end and I still can't get enough of you,' he said avidly, tracing a finger over my palm.

I felt like a fairytale princess.

He bent down and kissed me. It started off gently and then deepened as my heart rate went rocketing. He slid an arm around my waist, gently pulling me closer to him. His other hand slowly trailed down my neck, my shoulders and down the length of my arm.

I could feel goosebumps all over my skin, like it was

terribly cold. It was thrilling and electrifying. A small part of me wondered why I wasn't feeling all warm and secure and tranquil like I did when I was with Neel.

He slid his hands under my shirt and I felt them cold on my skin.

'What are you doing, Omi?' I asked him shakily. It was not fear that made it shaky, but anticipation and a burning desire for him to continue.

He looked at me, eyes wide.

And for some stupid reason, I felt guilty and pulled him close and touched my lips to his.

Until Neel stopped us.

Omi hit the ground face first, his arms twisting. However, he bounded onto his feet in a second. Neel looked like an enraged Spanish bull after he had hauled Omi off me.

And me? I sat up stunned, feeling shame and guilt.

A flash of light hit my eye and I jerked my head back. There was something in Neel's hand.

It was a long kitchen knife. And it looked even more honed and cruel when Neel clutched it tightly, shaking in rage or maybe anxiety.

The knife—it was for Omi ...

I had to stop this madness. Neel wasn't himself.

Neel looked lethal as he dodged Omi's punches and kicks and scored a hit every now and then. I could have never imagined peace-loving Neel thrashing someone right in front of my eyes and, least of all, that the *someone* would be Omi.

All I could do was scream like a lunatic, telling them to get off each other.

'Shut up! Stay out of this!' Neel barked at me, still not taking his focus off Omi.

I frantically looked around; no one else seemed to be around in the park. Where the hell did they all go?

Suddenly, I saw that I wasn't the only spectator.

There was a little girl standing on the other side of the grappling pair, watching fixedly. She seemed to be concentrating furiously on the two of them.

She wore a reddish frock and her jet-black hair was braided on either side of her head. Her eyes appeared completely still and black from where I stood, and strangely compelling.

It came to me in a flash.

Her face, complexion and her intensity—it was just like Omi.

No, this couldn't be.

I strode over to where she stood and opened my mouth to demand some answers.

Without a glance at my direction, she held up her hand to signal 'stop'. Her eyes were closed now and she was muttering something fervently, too faint for me to hear.

The fight was getting uglier by the second. Neel's lips were covered with blood, and blood flowed all over his face and down to his chin. He still held the knife firm.

Omi's state was worse. There was blood all over his face, and arms. I wanted to intervene, to stop them ...

'That wouldn't do any good.'

I snapped my head towards Sonali.

She had stopped her muttering and was looking at me as intently as she'd been studying the fight.

'Why are you here?' I blurted.

She looked back at the fight and jerked her head. 'To put an end to Omi,' she replied with finality.

She was helping Neel. I thought it strange; you'd want to stick with your own family, especially when you've been realms apart. Though suddenly, I remembered something Omi had told me last night:

The one person who loved me whom I sacrificed …

'Why?' I asked, puzzled. 'Did you set him up to kill Omi?'

'Yes. It was the only way. Omi does not belong here; you know it as well as I do. We need to kill him so that he doesn't find his way back to the Void. His essence needs to be put to rest.'

I swallowed. 'I don't think killing him is going to solve anything.' I shook my head stubbornly. How could I let the life be snuffed out of him after he'd come so far just to have a second chance at life, with me. That would be no different from what he did with Joanne.

No. Taking another life couldn't be the answer.

'He's as dead as I am, you know,' Sonali said coolly.

I shot her a disgusted look. 'Huh? Oh, he's alive. What is all this to you, anyway? Listen, why don't you just leave him alone and stop whatever freaky hold you have over Neel? I know he would never try to harm someone in his right mind.' Even I was surprised at how bitter I sounded.

She snorted. And I wanted to slap her right there and then.

'His mind has never been more right,' she said, puckering her eyebrows. Her breathing became rapid.

'What are you doing?' I asked.

'Stopping Omi from entering your boyfriend's head *and* trying to keep people away from this place *and* trying not to be distracted by you.'

I frowned. 'Can I help?' I squeaked, looking between her and the guys restlessly.

'No,' she replied and balled her fists, closing her eyes again.

Suddenly Neel struck a blow that left Omi staggering, dazed and disoriented, to the ground.

I wanted to run to him and cradle him on my lap. I wanted to shield him from Neel and then again, I wanted to protect Neel from being hurt any further. I wanted to stop this craziness.

I started to run towards them when Sonali caught my arm and hauled me back. 'Do you want another life to be taken? Because Neel is going to die if you try to stop anything that's going on here!'

I stared at her for a while. And then I dropped to my knees. 'Is it possible that I give up my own life so that Omi can have another chance?' I asked meekly, tears welling up.

This took her by surprise. 'Do you think that's going to stop them from throttling each other?' she said with dark humour.

'No, you didn't get what I meant. Is there a possibility that me dying could open up a way for him to become fully mortal with no connection to the other side?' I asked again.

She didn't say anything as it slowly sank in. Finally, she shook her head and said, 'No, it doesn't work that way.'

She pulled me up. 'The Void has no need for you. It is my essence that it has claimed, which of course, will never belong there. It is time we set my brother free from this darkness.'

Neel clutched the knife in one hand and held down Omi with the other. His face was calm and purposeful, like he knew exactly what he was doing. There was no panic or uncertainty as he took a deep breath and plunged the knife deep into Omi's chest, closing his eyes as Omi's shriek echoed around me.

I couldn't bear to look at Omi and instead fixed my gaze on Neel. He remained composed, though I knew what he was doing must be tearing him apart, as he held down a squirming Omi, not loosening his grip even as blood that was not his own spurted on his hands and on his face.

Omi's body had gone limp. As his breathing grew shallower, Omi Daan tilted his head towards me.

Mechanically, I crawled towards him, my vision blurred by tears and my ears hearing only the sound of my own sobbing.

His unwavering eyes were still on me when I reached him. His bloodied lips were quivering and I thought I saw a smile.

This was the second time I had to look into a pair of dead eyes knowing that, somehow, I was the one to blame. The guilt and grief that overwhelmed me was terrifying, I didn't want any comfort, I just yearned for emptiness.

A warm, slick hand touched me lightly on my arm, sending a slight tremor through me. I remembered the existence of

Neel beside me. Dazed, I looked up at his face. He looked like he was going to have a breakdown himself; I'd never seen him look so vulnerable. Tears and blood mingled on his face as he supported me.

'You did it.' Sonali was with us now.

I didn't know whether to thank her or curse her existence. Neel did that for me.

'Tha-tha-thank you,' he tried to tell her between his sobs.

Sonali nodded stiffly. 'I'm sorry you had to go through all that, but you did the right thing, Neel,' she said, giving him a sad smile. 'Don't worry about Omi. He's in a safer place now, both for him and everyone else.'

She looked around, and only then did I realise how dark it had become.

'I'll take care of everything here. You better get out of here before either of you have a nervous breakdown.'

We didn't stick around to see what happened next.

It took a long time to wash out all the blood from Neel's hands at the tap in a corner of the park. I splashed water on his face. Most of the blood had dried up. I wondered how much of the blood on him was his, and how much was Omi's. Shuddering, I tried to push away such horrifying thoughts.

After his face was clean, I checked his hands. He was still rubbing them vigorously though they were spotless. The look on his face was faraway and he kept chewing his lip nervously.

And my heart broke again. What was I putting him through? What if this changed him forever?

I slipped one hand through Neel's arm and clasped his hands, gently pulling them away from the running water. I turned off the tap with the other hand.

'Hey. They're clean now. We can go home,' I told him softly, managing an even tone.

'Home?' he asked, not taking his eyes off his hands. 'Home,' he repeated again and nodded, like he understood this time.

'Yes, home,' I sighed, shivering.

I helped him up and together we limped our way towards the park exit.

Epilogue

Another bolt of lightning strikes overhead as I skitter to a stop and try to get my bearings.

The land is dry and lifeless, as if it hasn't been inhabited for as long as could be remembered. There are no trees, no plants, not even shrubs, like one would find in a desert. The horizon is dark; massive, ominous clouds in contorted shapes loom overhead.

I can't remember how I got here but I know that I had been running, running for my life.

Something or someone had been stalking me. I could feel its presence, its wrath and its craving to get hold of me. Suddenly, its aura faded and I knew I was absolutely alone in this godforsaken place.

I clutch my head with my hands in despair. My heart keeps thudding louder and louder.

My lungs are protesting now; something in the air is starting to choke the life out of me. And as if trying to pry out whatever it was that was polluting my air bags, I dig my fingers into my chest in a desperate attempt.

Until I can breathe no more.

The desolate land turns upside down as I fall back, numb to the sharp pain that slowly spreads like warmth. The sky and the clouds seem to drift further and further away from me.

My vision blurs. I can no longer differentiate between land and sky. I hear the shrieking wind, angry and bitter, revelling in the dead space around me.

I groan and call for help to no one in particular.

And then I remember what to do.

I simply open my eyes.

'Neel? Neel, please wake up. Neel?' a voice washed over me.

A soft hand clutched mine, while another gently ran across my forehead, wiping away the beaded sweat. Her touch felt like home.

I lifted my eyes and met hers. I felt a calm that could come only from gazing into those eyes. My rapid breathing grew shallow, until air filled my lungs, wholesome and refreshing.

'Is it one of those nightmares again?' she asked before I could tell her I was okay now.

There was so much anguish in her eyes that I wanted to lie and say that it wasn't a nightmare. But lying to her was something I was never good at.

'Yes. Same as the previous one.'

My voice was hoarse and brittle at the same time. I hated how weak and fragile I was, after everything we had gone through. I hated seeing her blame and punish herself for my weakness.

To me, it seemed that son of a bitch had won after all.

And I could do nothing about it.

Three weeks of therapy for insomnia and I was better, though probably not as a result of the therapy since I never told my therapist the actual reason for my breakdown. I would wake up as early in the morning as I could and go for a jog, clearing up the cobwebs of the previous night's nightmare. The less sleep I managed, the safer my mind was. And because I kept myself awake for as long as I could at night, there were times when my brain would just shut down during the day.

And then the horrifying nightmares would plague me.

The bloody memories of driving a knife into his chest splattered my nightmares. Terrifying guilt would swarm me, followed by fear and then rage. The nightmare would smother me, suffocate me and bear me down until I remembered that little thing that Li told me, that little phrase which gave me a world of assurance and comfort and safety:

Just open your eyes.

Suzanne Sangi is seventeen years old, and doing her pre-university course in Mount Carmel College, Bangalore. She loves music, sings and plays the guitar. She started writing *Facebook Phantom* in the summer after her Class X board exams, when she was fifteen, and finished it the following summer.